D0439501

Sept 21
Total: 3
Last: 2015

THE RUNAWAY

THE RUNAWAY

GLEN HUSER

VANCOUVER   LONDON

Distribution and representation in Canada by
Fitzhenry & Whiteside • www.fitzhenry.ca

Distribution and representation in the UK by
Turnaround • www.turnaround-uk.com

Released in the USA in 2012

Mixed Sources
Cert no. SW-COC-001271
© 1996 FSC
FSC

Inside pages printed on FSC certified paper using vegetable-based inks.

Manufactured by Sunrise Printing
Manufactured in Chilliwack, BC, Canada in October 2010

2 4 6 8 10 9 7 5 3 1

Cataloguing-in-Publication Data for this book
is available from The British Library.

Library and Archives Canada Cataloguing in Publication

Huser, Glen, 1943-
The runaway / Glen Huser.

ISBN 978-1-896580-21-0

I. Title.

PS8565.U823R86 2011   jC813'.54   C2011-901036-4

For the True Blue Troupe:

Dianne

Glenys

& Raffaella (now gone, but ever with us)

Remembering the times—too brief—when the stage beckoned us.

Tradewind Books thanks the Governments of Canada and British Columbia for the financial support they have extended through the Canada Book Fund, Livres Canada Books, the Canada Council for the Arts, the British Columbia Arts Council and the British Columbia Book Publishing Tax Credit program.

 Canada Council for the Arts **Conseil des Arts du Canada**  BRITISH COLUMBIA ARTS COUNCIL
Supported by the Province of British Columbia

  LIVRES CANADA BOOKS

CHAPTER 1

*I*t's funny how years can go by as steady as telephone poles along a highway, with nothing but the bits and pieces of everyday life, and then, all of a sudden, a different kind of year will pop itself up and change everything. Topsy-turvy is what Pa would have called it. A topsy-turvy year.

I guess he'd had a couple of topsy-turvy years when he was a young man. He liked to talk about them—the year he was working in San Francisco and there was an earthquake that shook the city to pieces and left my dad running for a place as far away from mountains as he could find. Then there was the year before he and Ma got married when a twister carried away the house he was building for them—turned it into matchsticks that were left in a heap in the middle of Bentley's field three miles away.

But for me, up until the time that Pa died, life had been the bits-and-pieces, ordinary, everyday kind. Doing farm chores. Going to school. Hoeing the garden and swimming in Garvy's water hole in summer, skating on Oxbow Creek or sledding down Sprucetop Hill in winter. Learning some words of a play or a song for a Christmas concert. Helping Pa with his weekend auctioneering.

You know, sorting stuff into batches for him, writing down who owed what for which lot.

I've always been quick with a pencil. Not just writing, but sketching too; and somewhere along the line kids at school had taken to calling me "Doodlebug." So drawing was part of the bits and pieces too. Ma used to shake her head and go on about how it was harder to find a clean sheet of writing paper in her desk than finding raspberries in January. Like as not I had filled every piece with cartoons and doodles, and pictures of the cowboys I'd been reading about in the dime novels we traded one another as we ate our school lunches. Ma didn't approve of the dime novels, so at home in the evenings, I'd get my nose into a book by Mark Twain or Ma would read aloud to me from Charles Dickens or Baroness Orczy.

A pretty ordinary life, you'd have to agree. Well maybe the drawing was a bit unusual, but most everybody has something they can do a little better than other people. With Ma, it was singing. She had a way with a song—a jaunty one like "De Camptown Races" could make you feel like dancing, or something sad and slow like "Danny Boy" would bring a lump to your throat.

And Pa could tell a story to a crowd, in between his auctioning spiels, that would have everyone holding their sides with laughter. He could twist his voice into silly accents, and I can remember driving home from many an auction, the two of us talking like lunatics from who knows what country. "Zing me zat zong, Papa—zee one about Jozephine in zat flying mesheen?" I'd beg him, and he'd sing the whole song through in his most outrageous fracturing of English. I would have a chance later in my life to try this too, but I was never as good as Pa.

My best friend at school, Jimmy Bacon, could pitch a curveball that would tease the players from Huntsville into thinking it was as wild as a joker in rummy before it headed straight, smack-dab over the plate. We'd won most of our games since Jimmy started pitching.

These were the best pieces in the years that tumbled along uneventfully and finished off my first fourteen. But then, like I say, a year comes along when everything ordinary and everyday suddenly goes haywire. For me that was the year I turned fifteen.

First off there was the accident coming home from the auction at McBain's—an old couple retiring from farming and selling off pretty well everything. Ma had gone along to do the recording of the sales because I'd pleaded to be able to take my place as second baseman in a playoff with Huntsville.

The accident happened on a hill just a mile from our farm. There weren't many cars in Carrington County in 1922, so fate must've been working overtime to get two of them up at the top of that hill at the same time while the sun was just low enough to blind the encyclopedia salesman in his Reo and send him crashing into Pa's Model T.

I was in town celebrating our victory over Huntsville with Jimmy Bacon—Jimmy's dad had sprung for sodas at Carver's Drugstore—when the sheriff, Mr. McBride, found me. He told me that Pa must have been killed instantly. Ma was badly injured, and they'd taken her to the hospital over in Spirit Rapids.

I was crying so hard I couldn't see straight and I began running for home, but Mr. McBride and Mr. Bacon sent Jimmy after me.

"Leroy, no sense to you going back to that empty house." Mr. Bacon fished a hankie out of his jacket pocket and handed it to me. "You come on home with us."

I could see Jimmy was trying hard to keep his own tears back.

"I'll send someone over to tend to the animals." Sheriff McBride shook his head sadly. It was like he already knew that pretty well everything we owned, including our three cows and our team of plough horses, would end up being sold at auction not long after Pa was buried and Ma was released from the Spirit Rapids hospital in a wheelchair.

The auctioneer was from Spirit Rapids and was nowhere near as good as Pa—everyone said so. By the time all of Pa's bills had been paid off and the bank reclaimed the farm, we didn't have much to our name. In addition to the stuff from her dresser drawer and closet, Ma had her songbooks and a little portable pump organ, the pictures off our walls and some bits of china. Everything I owned I could fit into a carpet bag—my clothes, my pencils and drawing paper, some of my sketches in a folder I'd made that Ma had covered in oilcloth for me, a few books. I put in Pa's hairbrush and his razor and shaving mug. If I looked really hard in the mirror, sometimes I thought I could see a mustache about ready to spring forth.

It wasn't much we had on the platform of the Carrington railway station.

"You mustn't be nervous, Leroy," my mother said, smiling up at me from where she sat in her wheelchair. She was concerned because I'd broken out in a rash and couldn't stop scratching at my wrists, which were sticking out from the sleeves of my best jacket, an article of clothing that had either shrunk since Christmas or else I'd grown a few inches.

I *was* nervous. We were headed four counties over to stay with my Aunt Alvina, who, out of charity, had invited us to come and live on the farmstead where Ma had grown up. Alvina was the widow of Ma's only brother, Hiram, and she had two sons, Albert and Virgil. They were grown men who, on Uncle Hiram's death, had taken over the family business—the Cutter's Creek Livery Barn and Harness Store.

"Maybe I should go off somewhere and get work," I said to Ma, "and when I've saved up enough money, I could send for you."

"Oh, Leroy, my sweet boy." She reached up and clasped my hand. "There will be all kinds of ways you can help there. Your cousins are hard-working, pious men. And you need to go to school. You just need to be a good boy. It will all work out beautifully."

Ma was an optimist. But the train whistle, as the locomotive rounded the bend outside of Carrington, sounded doleful in my ears. And when I first glimpsed Virgil waiting in the buggy at the Jackson Junction station, his shaggy eyebrows drawn together in a frown and his mouth set in a grim line did nothing to put my mind at ease.

I think he tried to soften his expression as he greeted me, but I found myself scratching away at a surge of itchiness on my arms. The conductor got Ma's wheelchair down from the coach, and Virgil went into the train and collected her in his arms, carrying her like a child down to the platform. It looked like no effort for him. He was a huge man. For Ma, he tipped his mouth up into a smile as he settled her into the buggy, placing her wheelchair in the back with her.

"You all comfortable, Aunt Melinda? We got a ways to go to Cutter's Creek. Leroy, put that extra cushion in behind your ma. Support her back better."

Guiding me onto the driver's seat with him, Virgil got the team moving. "Gee-up, Spit, gee-up, Polish."

Spit and Polish. Could it be that the brothers had a touch of humour?

Ma kept a conversation going on the long ride to Cutter's Creek, remembering places along the way where she and Hiram had picked blueberries when they were youngsters, picnicked at a popular swimming hole and in the winter had skating parties along Cutter's Creek itself. Virgil's responses were mostly grunts and, the odd time, a loquacious "You don't say." I could see no trace of gentleness or a smile as he kept his gaze on the rumps of Spit and Polish, or gave me a glance from the corner of his eye.

Aunt Alvina hugged me when we got to the farmhouse and noted, "You're taller than your Pa ever got to be. Must take after the Grimble side of the family. You got the Grimble's chestnut-coloured hair too. Just like your Uncle Hiram's, although his weren't so curly."

Ma gave me a little encouraging smile, and I handed Aunt Alvina a picture I'd painted for her from a photograph of Uncle Hiram. In the photograph he hadn't been smiling. But in the transfer to a piece of art, I tipped the corners of his mouth up a bit.

"Well, ain't that something." Aunt Alvina held the picture closer to the light coming in through the kitchen window. "Will you take a look at this, Virg?"

Virgil took the painting from her and studied it. "Yes. Mighty fine," he muttered. "We'll have to put you to painting some new signs for the harness shop. Bet you'd be really handy at that."

Aunt Alvina put the picture up on a ledge beside some canisters. "I'll be able to look at that, Leroy, whenever I'm working at the counter."

"Why don't you take a half hour's rest and grab a bite to eat before I take you into Cutter's Creek with me?" he said.

He nodded in my direction as he eased himself onto a chair by the kitchen table.

"I thought he could wait until next week to register at the school," Ma said. "Give him a little time to get his bearings."

"My thoughts exactly." Virgil signalled his mother to pour him a cup of coffee. "I'll take him into town, and he can just help us around the harness shop, maybe lend a hand at the livery stable."

"God sees the little sparrow fall," Aunt Alvina began to sing as she checked a pot simmering on the stove. "It meets his tender view . . ."

CHAPTER 2

I think I felt like the little sparrow Aunt Alvina was singing about in the trip from the farm into Cutter's Creek, except I wasn't so certain God had his eye on me. Albert did, though, as soon as I was dropped off at the harness shop. This cousin, I was to discover, only had one eye. The other was glass, and its colour, cornflower blue, didn't quite match that of his working eye, which was more like the shade of a sky that was getting set to rain.

Albert fixed his eye on me as Virgil headed to the livery with the horse and buggy. "The Lord has placed you in our hands, Cousin Leroy," Albert said from his perch behind the store's counter. "It is an abiding trust. You know what is said about idle hands—they are the work of the Devil. We shall see that the Devil is kept far from your fingers, boy. There's a list of chores to be done that we'll keep tacked to the wall in the back room. As you work through the chores, you can mark them off."

I looked Albert in his one eye and asked, "What is my pay to be?"

Albert didn't say anything at first. He just got down off his stool behind the cash register and walked around the end of the counter to where I was standing. He grabbed hold of my arms, one in each hand, and shook me mightily. When he was finished my head was spinning and I felt like my legs had turned to rubber. I staggered back a couple of steps.

"Love of money is the root of all evil," Albert lisped. "I expect you to remember that. You will work for your bed and board, and to pay off what your father owed us."

"We paid it!" I could feel tears beginning to well and shook my head to keep them back. "Ma sent you what was left after the auction—"

Albert put a finger to his lips. "Heed your words, boy, and be thankful I am in a clement mood today. Do you see that hickory stick leaning against the wall by the saddles there?"

He helped me direct my gaze by spinning me a half turn.

"It is what we shall turn to, should we encounter insubordination. Spare the rod . . ."

"I'll tell my ma."

Virgil stepped up behind me and put one of his huge hands around the back of my neck. "You could add to the grief of your ma," he said, his voice, unctuous and hollow, slipping past his crooked teeth. "She's lost a husband and you would burden her. Your father still owed us money. We are family and we did not begrudge him a loan, although he was a weak man . . ."

"He wasn't!" I struggled away from Virgil's grasp and lunged into Albert, whose one eye looked at me with the baleful glare of a polecat disturbed at his dinner.

"He was a weak man," Albert repeated, "and your work today will rub the tiniest edge off what he owed us."

"That car of his. Such foolishness," Virgil grumbled.

I felt like crying but I was determined not to show them another tear.

And so began a period of indentured slavery that lasted for over a year. The cousins had a hired man—Eben, an old bachelor—and it became my job before breakfast and after school to give him a hand with the chores and to work at the livery stables all day Saturday. Eben didn't seem too happy with my presence even though I was relieving him of much of the work he must have done all on his own before Ma and I came to live at Cutter's Creek. I couldn't help thinking that my cousins must have cut back some of his wages, with my appearance on the scene.

I did my best not to let Ma know how unhappy I was, but of course it didn't take her long to figure out that things weren't exactly jake here at Cutter's Creek.

"You're missing your pa, aren't you?" she said, one of those evenings when we happened to be alone in the parlour.

I nodded my head but didn't trust myself to try and say anything.

"I miss him terribly too." She sighed and put down some mending she'd been doing for Aunt Alvina. "And you're working so hard."

I bit my lip.

"You've had to grow up all of a sudden. I wish . . ." But she left her wish hanging unformed as Virgil and Albert came in with their newspapers and lit up their pipes. It was their routine—a half hour in the parlour armchairs, papers rustling, the odd, terse comment about the weather or the market yield for crops, once in a while a question directed to my mother. When Aunt Alvina came in from the kitchen, it would signal time for prayers.

My cousins put on pious faces and gathered Ma into the evening circle, fussing over the sweet way she read a Bible passage and admiring her skill at the pump organ that was in a corner of the parlour. I knew Ma was grateful that, while the accident had wrecked her legs for walking, she was still able to work the pedals of the organ. Often over prayers, I would find myself nodding off from my day's labours. If this happened while Ma had her back to us, I would be prodded awake with a severe thump to my skull by one of Virgil's huge-knuckled fingers, levered into action with his thumb.

When summer vacation came, my hours at the harness shop and livery were increased. There were days when I felt my Grimble cousins were hard-pressed to find something for me to do. So I'd end up reshining the metal fittings on horse tackle that I'd polished only two days before, or grooming a horse whose hair was in way better condition than my own. I'd heard more than one customer declare the livery stable the cleanest barn on the prairie.

One summer day I'd finished everything on the chore list by noon, and Virgil, who was taking his turn in the livery, decided to treat himself to dinner at the restaurant in the Cutter's Creek Hotel down the street.

My fingers had been itching to pick up a pencil and do some drawing. When school had been on I'd managed to find some time, after I'd finished my assignments, to use the back pages of a scribbler for doodling. Now that it was summer vacation, I hadn't even been able to do that, but with some of the optimism I must have inherited from my mother, I packed a half-used scribbler around with me, telling the brothers when they eyed it with suspicion that I wanted to keep in practice doing arithmetic problems, should I have some spare minutes.

Under their watchful gazes, spare minutes had been as rare as sleigh bells in July. But today the livery was spotless and quiet, and I was the only one there apart from Spit and Polish, the dray team of Clydesdales, a couple of riding horses and an Appaloosa that had been left by a visitor who'd gone fishing with his brother up the creek.

I smoothed a page at the back of my scribbler and sharpened a pencil to a fine point using my pocket knife. The Appaloosa in his stall was a perfect model—I think he was asleep on his feet. I shaded in his spots, some as light as a mouse's skin, some dark as a crow's feather. I was pleased with the flow of the line that caught the slight curve of his back and the intricacies of his hind legs. Where his hide was lightest, I cross-hatched the darkness of the stable wood behind him so it showed up in relief.

As I reviewed the result, my only wish was that the scribbler page hadn't been lined. If you could forget about the lines, it was a mighty fine drawing of an Appaloosa. Once I had a pencil in my hand, I was not content with filling just one free page. I moved on to the next, and on this one some devilment took hold of me—I did a sketch of the Grimble brothers leaning back idly against some bales of hay. I sketched Albert chewing on a piece of barley grass with his snaggleteeth showing. I had him using one hand to play toss and catch with his glass eye. I was embellishing the dome of Virgil's head with a few wiry strands of hair when I sensed someone standing behind where I was perched on the edge of a bin of oats.

It was Albert.

"Let me see," he said.

I tried to flip back to the page with the Appaloosa, but Albert's thumb caught on the cartoon.

"Do you recollect our little talk about idle hands some time ago?" He ripped the page out of the scribbler.

When I didn't answer, he directed me to go across to the harness shop, collect the hickory stick and bring it back over to the stable.

"It's not a picture of anyone in particular," I protested. "Just a couple of cowpokes . . ."

Albert looked at me sternly and pointed toward the door.

I came very close to hurling the stick as far as it would go and taking off. But where would I go? And when they caught up with me, things would be even worse. I could feel my heart beating high in my throat as I returned to the livery.

Out of the corner of my eye, I could see Virgil coming back from the restaurant. Albert spied him too and waited until his brother was in the barn before he showed him my drawing and suggested what he envisioned to be an appropriate punishment.

"No," I pleaded. "I'll never draw a picture of you again. You can tear this one up and make me eat the pieces."

"You hold him, Virgil," Albert said.

That's when I decided to run, but Virgil's hands were quick and in an instant he had the upper part of my body in a vice-like grip.

"Go over to the railing, take hold of it and bend over."

I resigned myself to the beating and did what he said.

The first thwack of the hickory stick against the seat of my britches made me cry out in pain. The Appaloosa snorted and reared, and a couple of the other horses whinnied. I bit my lip rather than wail out again, and I could taste blood. I found myself counting the whacks—there were six before Albert stopped. But he continued to beat the stick against one of the barn supports for a couple of minutes, perhaps as a reminder of what lay in store for me, should I misbehave again.

That's when I decided that I *would* run away. But it wouldn't be on the spur of the moment. It would be a planned escape.

Ma knew something bad must have happened because I'd skipped dinner and asked to be excused from prayers. I went straight up to my room. As I lay on my bed, reliving the events of the day, the mumbling of the evening prayers and the soft music of Ma at the organ seeped through the floorboards. A little while later I heard the heavy tread of one of the cousins carrying her up to her bedroom. Then there was the slighter sound of Aunt Alvina's shuffle as she came up and helped Ma ready herself for sleep. A few minutes later there was a rap on my door. I went to the door and opened it a crack.

"I know you're not feeling well," Aunt Alvina whispered, "but your mama would like it if you came in and said good night to her."

As I made my way down the hall to Ma's room, I could hear my aunt humming "Onward, Christian Soldiers," the tune growing fainter with her descent of the stairs.

Ma was sitting up in bed, propped up against the pillows. She beckoned me over and took my hand.

"What's troubling you, son?" she asked.

All I could come up with was a kind of choking noise.

Ma rubbed her fingers back and forth over my hand, her gaze never wavering from my face.

I finally managed to get something out. "Ma, do we owe them money?"

"Alvina and the boys?"

I nodded my head.

"No, dear. With the sale of the farm I was able to pay off what we owed the boys on the car, and Virgil put what was left over—it wasn't much—in the bank for safekeeping."

"Virgil has our money! How much?"

"A couple hundred dollars. Hiram always said this would be a home for me if I needed one. Your grandfather left him the farm. That's the way it was done in those days. A son inherited the farm; a daughter got married and made her own life."

I closed my eyes for a moment. There was murder in my heart as I thought of Virgil with all of Pa's hard-earned money.

"That will be your money," Ma said, "when you're ready to go out into the world. One day . . ."

I could see Ma looking very weary. I kissed her good night.

Somehow, I thought as I headed back to my room, someway I'll get what's mine and the getting of it will be a righteous and sweet revenge. Didn't the Bible have something to say about an eye for an eye?

Albert would need to be careful, I thought as I smiled in spite of the pain still radiating from where my body had received the brunt of the beating. He only had one eye.

CHAPTER 3

Summer vacation ended and I returned, with some relief, to school. I felt fortunate that we had a new ninth-grade instructor, Miss Blanchard, who wasn't keen about walking around the room much. Some of the boys in class were close in age to her, and since she was curvaceous and comely, they practically fell out of their chairs ogling her. She directed our lessons from the front of the room, and this allowed me greater access to the back of my scribbler where I'd taken to hiding a few sheets of drawing paper. My desk-mate, Lemuel Snodgrass, had his own covert activity—reading dime novels concealed at the back of one of his books—so we were well matched and not into snitching on one another.

I continued to consider prospects for running away, particularly as the brothers found more occasions to exercise the hickory stick.

As the school months wore on, most of my waking moments and much of my dreamtime were focused on the primary obstacles to my plan. First there was the concern about leaving my mother who was growing more frail. More and more often she chose not to leave her upstairs bedroom.

When winter set in, once I'd finished my chores, I'd hurry up to her room with her supper tray.

Ma would smile and say something sweet like, "You smell like fresh snow," and while she toyed with her food, I'd talk about my day or the world beyond the farmhouse. Just the good stuff—such as Duke, the old collie dog, chasing snowballs like a puppy, or the willow by the gate, all covered with ice crystals and looking like a fancy chandelier.

O n Christmas Day my mother joined everyone in the parlour. Gifts were as scarce as laughter at a Grimble Christmas. But before Ma had dressed and gone down, I went into her room and gave her a little sketch I'd done of Pa that I'd put in a frame fashioned from willow pieces and painted with some gold paint Miss Blanchard had at school.

"Oh my," Ma said, holding the picture out in front of her for a long minute. "What a perfect Christmas gift. Do you recollect how much Pa loved Christmas? He was always bringing home anyone he ran across who didn't have a place to go. I never knew who to expect—but we had such wonderful times."

"Yes, and he'd get us all laughing until our sides ached."

For a minute it seemed that I could hear Pa right there, telling tales in his funny-stories accent.

Then it all faded.

Ma reached over to her bed table and handed me a small package wrapped in tissue and tied with one of her hair ribbons.

"It's not much . . ."

I opened the package carefully. Inside there was a tan-coloured paisley neckerchief with my initials embroidered on one corner.

"I love it!" I tied it around my neck and modelled it for her. But I took it off before I went downstairs and I wasn't surprised that Ma said nothing of the sketch I'd given her when she joined us in the parlour.

She'd applied some rouge to add colour to her cheeks, and I could see a disapproving look on Albert's face. Both Albert and Virgil could go on at length about the evils of painted women. She wore the green velvet dress she'd worn for Christmases for as long as I could remember, but I could see it hung loosely on her now, her hands almost lost in the sleeves.

"Play us a Christmas hymn on the organ, Melinda," Aunt Alvina suggested after we'd spent a fair bit of the day on Bible readings and prayers.

"Maybe another time," Ma said, and I felt the cold grip of what this response meant—that she wasn't strong enough to honour the request.

Aunt Alvina reached over, patted Ma's hand and started singing "Hark! The Herald Angels Sing." We joined in, but I had to strain to hear Ma's voice—as soft as the brush of angels' wings.

Another thing that worried me about running away was the money I would need to begin a new life. I had a feeling that the brothers would sooner paint their faces and dance a jig on Sunday than give me any of the two hundred dollars Ma had entrusted to them. So I began calculating the wages that should have been coming to me over the past year, and I nearly made myself ill trying to conceive of ways to pry some of it loose from my parsimonious cousins.

There was always a bit of money in the cash register, but whichever brother was behind the counter never strayed far from it. And every Friday Virgil took the money to the bank. I wondered where he kept it throughout the week—locked up in the roll-top desk in the parlour, or hidden someplace in his upstairs bedroom?

One night when I heard the boys rattling the rafters with their snores, I got up and checked out the roll-top desk by candlelight. But the drawers yielded nothing more than old bills of sale, tax receipts, some tintype photographs, letters and postcards.

I couldn't work up the nerve to search Virgil's room in the dark. But an opportunity came unexpectedly one day. Albert was driving Doctor Masefield out to the farmhouse to see my mother, who had taken a turn for the worse, so he picked me up after school.

While the doctor was examining Ma in her bedroom, Albert was in the barn with Eben, probably checking to see that I was keeping on top of all my chores.

Aunt Alvina told me to get the fresh laundry and take it up to my cousins' rooms. She handed me two piles of clothing wrapped in different-patterned nightshirts. "You take that white one up to Albert's room. Goes in the bottom drawer of his chiffonier. And the striped—that's Virgil's. His is the second drawer."

I did as she bid, saving Virgil's laundry for the last, distributing his socks and union suits, pressed shirts and nightshirts among similar items in the second drawer. Quickly I checked the bottom drawer of the chiffonier. This seemed to be reserved for summer clothes. In the top drawer, though, there were odds and ends—a pennant from Kansas City, a canister of talcum powder, a buttonhook, a harmonica. Who'd have thought a harmonica! I wondered if Virgil had ever played it.

Alongside the harmonica was a rosewood box about the size of one of Ma's songbooks. I tried to lift it out, but it must have been screwed right into the wood of the drawer bottom. It had a decorative clasp with a keyhole centred in it. No key—but it was unlocked. Opening the lid, I found a small wad of money neatly bound with a piece of elastic. Envelopes were filled with coins of different denominations.

So this is where he keeps the week's earnings.

I heard a door close down the hall. I hurriedly dropped the lid, slipped the clasp back into place, closed Virgil's top drawer and made my way out of his bedroom. The doctor had come out of Ma's room. When he spotted me, he shook his head. I could see he was prepared to give me a message that wouldn't be good news.

"She's sleeping and will for some time with the draft I've given her," he said, putting his hand on my shoulder. "She may rally. But she may not. It's mostly just spirit that's holding her together. I've left some medicine on her dresser. Two teaspoons mixed in a small glass of lukewarm water. Not more often than every four hours."

Ma slept through dinner and evening prayers.

When everyone had gone to bed, I pulled the top blanket from my own bed, tiptoed down the hall, curled into an old easy chair in the corner of her room and wrapped the blanket around me. I woke, shivering. Ma, I could see, was lying in bed with her eyes open.

Disentangling myself from my blanket, I hurried over and reached for her hand. Even before I touched it, I knew that she was already gone. I hoped it was to a place where she would be able to run free again, a place where she'd be reunited with my father.

CHAPTER 4

At Ma's graveside, Aunt Alvina sang a hymn, and the coffin was lowered into an opening chipped out of the March earth, which was only beginning to thaw. Aunt Alvina's voice wasn't a patch on Ma's, though, and I tried to shut out the sound and bring to mind how Ma would have sung "And He walks with me and He talks with me . . ."

For a few weeks I was grief-struck and couldn't muster myself to think of anything much except how to get through each day. But as summer drew nearer and the prospect loomed of slaving for the brothers all the way through vacation, my sadness was displaced by a firm resolve to clear out. It struck me that after I finished the ninth grade my cousins might yank me out of school for good.

I couldn't help thinking of the two hundred dollars Ma had given Virgil to bank. By rights it was mine now. One day as I was working in the harness shop and Virgil was behind the till, exercising his eyes by watching me, I summoned up the courage to ask him about it.

Virgil paused in the business of picking his teeth with a metal toothpick he always kept handy, and snorted. "From what we've been putting out for your provisions, I'd say it's more likely you're owing us that amount."

"I work for my room and board."

"Then get on with it, boy. All those saddles need a good working over."

I gritted my teeth and continued on with my chores. But I kept an eye on the harness sales. Business was slow, so I waited for a week with better takings. It finally came.

Albert's one good eye glistened with the pleasure the ringing of the cash register brought him as a couple of families moving onto farms just outside Cutter's Creek outfitted their teams and riding horses. A well-to-do town family left their team and a healthy deposit while they were on a jaunt with friends, motoring across a couple of states and up into Canada. The fisherman had left his Appaloosa again, and the Clydesdales with the dray wagon had been rented out several times when Thursday rolled around.

It's said that a watched kettle never boils, and I swear, as I waited and listened that evening in late May, it took forever for the brothers to settle into their nighttime snores. About half an hour after Aunt Alvina's quavering lullaby to herself of "Shall We Gather at the River?" had faded away, I got up. I had dressed in my best clothes earlier and had pulled just a blanket over me, should anyone have found occasion to peer into my room. In my carpet bag I'd gathered a few possessions I felt I couldn't leave behind—a photograph of Ma and Pa on their wedding day, a snapshot of myself on my thirteenth birthday, my portfolio of drawings with the oilcloth cover Ma had so carefully stitched, and Pa's toiletries. A change of clothes. I'd also snuck a hunk of cheese, half a loaf of bread and a few cookies from Aunt Alvina's pantry, wrapping them in a clean napkin. I pushed the bag well under my bed.

When the house was quiet except for the ticking of the grandfather clock in the upstairs hall, I crept out of my room. Albert's door was ajar, but Virgil's was shut.

What if Virgil locked his door at night?

When I tested the doorknob, it turned, and with the slightest push the door opened with only a very small creak.

A shaft of moonlight spilled over the floor at the foot of Virgil's bed, and there was enough illumination that I was able to tiptoe to the chiffonier without bumping into his wooden clothes butler or the easy chair angled against a braided rug. I was relieved to find the rosewood box in the top drawer just where I expected it to be. When I tried to open the box, though, the lid refused to budge. It must have been just happenstance that I'd found it unlocked before.

It took me a couple of minutes to regulate my breath. Common sense told me that the key must not be far away. I closed my eyes and envisioned Virgil adding today's money to the box, locking it and—where would he put the key? Into a trouser pocket? The inside pocket of his jacket? I went over to the wooden butler and checked out these possibilities. Nothing. I carefully explored the items on top of the chiffonier. A hairbrush and a comb. A dish with some collar buttons. His watch and fob.

An image of Virgil checking his watch and then returning it to a pocket in the vest that covered his portly belly came to mind.

There had been no vest with the clothing on the butler. And then I saw it, draped over an arm of the chair. I came close to squealing with delight when my fingers came upon a small key in the vest's right-hand pocket. My hand was shaking as I tried it in the keyhole of the rosewood box. A wiggle to the right and then back to the left, and I heard the welcome click of the lock releasing. The roll of bills inside was twice as fat as the one I'd handled before. I shoved it into one of my jacket pockets and the envelopes of coins into another.

Was it more than the amount Ma had entrusted to him? I wasn't about to stop and count it. Cautiously I made my way back to my room and eased the carpet bag out from under the bed. In a few minutes I was outside. The Grimble farmyard was awash in moonlight. Duke crawled out from under the porch, a puzzled look on his face. I gave him a scratch behind the ears, and he followed at my heels as I made my way to the barn.

Spit and Polish were in their stalls. My plan was to ride Polish into Jackson Junction and then leave him tethered with a note: *This horse is the property of Virgil and Albert Grimble. Please notify them by a telegram to Cutter's Creek.*

Polish was a plodding beast, but once I got him saddled and we were out on the road he seemed to gather energy and had more bounce in his stride. I wondered if he had once been a saddle horse and was being reminded of a younger, happier time, not simply bound to the tiresome trip from the farm into town and back, day after day, year after year.

As I urged Polish onto the main road, Duke followed for a short way until I hollered at him to go on home. How long would it take me to get to Jackson Junction and its railway line? I tried to remember the length of the trip in the buggy when Virgil picked Ma and me up at the station and drove us to the farm. It seemed like many hours, but the trip should be much faster with Polish trotting along free from the buggy.

I figured that once my Grimble cousins found me missing,

they'd waste no time in raising an alarm. They wouldn't know for sure that I'd be headed for the nearest railway town, but they'd likely make that a good guess. They would probably call the sheriff in Jackson Junction. Or maybe one of them would come after me. All I knew was that I had to put as much distance between the brothers and me as possible.

As I rode toward Jackson Junction, the sun began to wash over farmers' fields, patches of wood and scrubland. My mind was a-swirl about whether or not to wait for a passenger train and get a proper ticket to somewhere a good length down the line. But then I remembered seeing hoboes riding the freights through Carrington when my friends and I played along the rail yards even though we'd been cautioned to stay away. Maybe I could stow away on one.

After a couple of hours I rested Polish at the spot where Ma said she once picnicked, and eagerly counted the money in my pockets. There was eighty-seven dollars in bills and just over twelve dollars in change. It was only about half of Ma's money but it would stand me in good stead for quite a while.

I remounted Polish and rode him for another hour, but by that time I was fighting sleep and even came close to falling off the old buggy horse. Coming to a meadow bordered by a forested area, I guided Polish into the woods and tied his reins to a tree. I unfastened my carpet bag from the saddle and propped it against a cottonwood trunk, using it as a headrest, though a very uncomfortable one. The grass beneath the tree was damp with dew, and I found myself eyeing a pine some distance away. It proved drier, and I was able to wedge the carpet bag between two huge roots. Curling against it I fell asleep.

Somewhere in my slumber, I fell into a dream. I was riding

Polish, but Pa was beside me riding Spit, and we were cantering down a country road.

"Thees ol' grey mare she ain't what she useta be," Pa was singing in his silly accent.

He was a bit ahead of me, and as he tapped his heels into Spit's sides, she began to run.

"Wait for me, Pa!" I hollered, and used my own heels to get Polish to go faster, but he stopped and whinnied.

The whinnying woke me up.

For a minute I couldn't remember where I was, and then I sat up and looked through the trees to where I'd tethered Polish.

And there stood Albert, dismounted from his own horse— not Spit. He must have gone into town for a faster one. He was holding Polish's reins and was looking around to see where I was.

"Boy! You better get yourself over here."

I grabbed my carpet bag, eased myself around to the other side of the pine tree, and began crawling into a dense thicket just beyond.

"Horse thievery!" Albert was hollering. "Men have been hung for that, y'know. Now quit hiding and get yourself out here."

I was deep inside the thicket and could no longer see Albert, so I hoped he was unable to spot me. But I could still hear him.

"Come on out and take your medicine!"

I'd never heard such rage in a person's voice. And I could hear his horse crashing through the underbrush, closer and closer to the thicket.

"You ain't going to get away, boy." Albert continued to shout. "No one steals money and property from a Grimble. I'll hunt you down, and you'll wish you'd never been born to break the Lord's commandment."

But I think the Lord was on my side that day. The willow brush became even thicker, and I worked my way along it, finally coming onto a marshy stream. I kept moving along it, at times plunging into bog mud up to my shins.

Finally the creek-side scrub brush tangled with the barbed wire of a farm fence, and I made my way cautiously along it even though it took me by an open field. I could see farm buildings in the distance and—yes!—the highway beyond. So now all I had to do was manage to keep out of Albert's sight the rest of the way into town.

CHAPTER 5

It was a long walk, and I kept a wary eye out for the sight of a figure on horseback leading a riderless horse. Every step, I watched for places that might offer quick hideaways.

As the day wore on, I finished off the food I'd packed. By noon there was more traffic on the road and at times I was tempted to hail someone in a wagon or a buggy and ask for a ride, or put out a hitchhiker's thumb as a car approached. But caution won out over my sore feet, and I slipped away into whatever ditch I could find whenever I spotted another traveller.

With such slow progress, I didn't get into Jackson Junction until late afternoon. I remembered the main street with its few stores, a blacksmith shop and a town hall. What else was there? It would be risky to allow myself much exposure on the main thoroughfare, but before ducking into a side street, I picked out a bank, a Harvey House restaurant, a barbershop and the sheriff's office.

The sheriff's office set my heart racing and sent me hurrying toward the train station. On a side street I saw a woman putting a pie out on a window ledge to cool, and my stomach rumbled. I could see her watching me from the window and then she stepped out onto the porch, a rolling pin held like a weapon in one hand. I hurried on.

From the next corner, I saw the station and the stockyards another block south. For a few minutes I agonized over whether or not to go inside to check the train schedule. Would the station agent have been alerted to look for a sixteen-year-old runaway? There was no sign of a train or anyone waiting on the platform.

My stomach rumbled again. I had to eat.

The Harvey House had a high false front, and I could pick it out over the rooftops. I was thankful it was a block over from the sheriff's office. Once I was around the corner, it was only a few steps to the entrance of the restaurant. The head waiter looked down his nose at my mud-crusted boots and trouser cuffs, gave me a menu and tucked me away at a table in a far corner.

At times, on his auction circuit, Pa and I had stopped for a restaurant meal. Pa always joked with the waiters, his laughter bringing smiles to those seated around us. At a large table next to me, there was a gathering of people Pa would have enjoyed. A fat man who seemed to be presiding over the group was given to bursts of explosive laughter. Between mouthfuls, a young girl sang a couple of lines of a song as if in answer to a question that had been raised. She had a sweet voice that made me think of Ma. The youngest in the group, she had an abundance of strawberry blonde curls. A white shirtwaist with a small black bow at the collar served to heighten the delicate hue of her complexion—the rosy blush of her lips and cheeks.

"Why don't you take a picture?" the fat man asked, loud enough for everyone in the restaurant to hear. A chuckle rippled through the group.

By this time a waitress had made her way over to where I was sitting. "Don't pay them any attention," she said, pulling a pad from her apron pocket. "They're Chautauqua actors celebrating their last day in town."

"Chautauqua?"

"You know—the big tent show. They've been here for a week. That big bell-ringer is always chucking quips at anyone who'll listen. What'll you have, dearie?"

"Chicken with all the trimmings, please. Say, you wouldn't happen to know when the trains are coming through today, would you?"

"The passenger trains have come and gone, both east and west."

"Any freights?"

"Don't really know their schedule. Stock train should be here sometime tomorrow. You look mighty young to be shipping livestock."

"Just checking. For my uncle."

"You want to wash up?"

I guess I must have appeared like someone who'd been shook up in a bag of dust, after my day on the road.

I used my boot to push my carpet bag out of sight under the table. In the washroom I spent a few minutes working off some of the dried mud. My money was secure in my jacket pockets, but I kept a close eye on my coat, draped on a door peg, as I rolled up my sleeves, soaped my hands and washed my face.

With most of the grime gone from my skin, my clothes dusted off and my hair slicked down as much as my curls would permit, I tucked into the hefty helping of fried chicken and potatoes the waitress brought me. I was so busy putting myself on the outside of this meal that I didn't notice anyone else entering the restaurant. But when I drew breath and stopped to wipe my mouth with my napkin, I happened to glance up to where the head waiter was busily engaged in a conversation with someone who had just come into the restaurant.

Albert.

At the same instant I spied him, he spotted me.

Both of us froze for a couple of seconds. I quickly reached under the table for my carpet bag, but somehow it had gotten stuck between a table leg and a crosspiece of wood in the table's underpinnings.

"There he is!" Albert roared. "Thief!"

A woman in a large straw hat uttered a scream. A couple of men at other tables leaped to their feet.

I abandoned my carpet bag and raced toward the rear door next to the washing-up room.

"Stop! Thief!" Albert hollered, as I lunged through the door into the alley.

CHAPTER 6

Panic-stricken, I ran to the end of the block, galloping across Main Street and south toward the railway tracks. I hoped there might be some woods where I might hide out until a freight pulled in.

As I neared the tracks, I saw a couple of rail cars with CHAUTAUQUA lettered on their sides. Three young men were loading piles of canvas onto the freight car. When their backs were turned, I slipped behind a shed. It took a few minutes to get my heart to settle down. Was Albert right behind me?

From my hiding place, I watched the men work. On the platform were trunks and crates, stacks of folding chairs and a piano. The young men had the look of college boys like ones I'd seen in Carrington working at summer jobs.

"I don't know about you guys . . ." One of the workers stopped, removed his cap and wiped his brow with a handkerchief. "But I'm famished."

"I could eat a horse," another said.

They tramped off toward the Harvey House.

Now was my chance. I dashed across the tracks and hoisted

myself up into the car. Canvas had been packed quite tightly into one half of the baggage car, and there was a heap of what I figured must be tent poles to climb over. But I was able to make my way to the back and even found a spot where it was possible for me to sit down. A shaft of dim light streamed through a piece of broken board just above me.

I hadn't been seated two minutes, though, when I heard someone clambering into the car.

Whillikers! Was I to have no luck?

It must be Albert!

I quickly pulled a bit of free-flapping canvas over me, but it wasn't quite big enough. It had a paraffin smell that almost made me gag. I could hear whomever it was scrambling along toward the back of the car. He was getting closer and closer. I held my breath.

Then I felt a hand brush my face. I yelped. At the same time I heard a loud gasp. I threw off the canvas and saw a hobo kneeling a few inches away from me. He had matted hair, a grime-streaked face and eyes as large as saucers. I must have looked like I was ready to yell out again because he covered my mouth with his hand.

We both listened. But we couldn't hear anyone talking or moving.

"You gave me a start," the man said, removing his hand. He edged a bit closer. There was a smell of unwashed clothing, bad breath and sweat. He smiled, revealing several gaps among his front teeth.

"And who have we here, riding the rods, casting his fate to chance and the yard police?" He chuckled softly.

"Um . . . Lemuel," I said, thinking of my deskmate at school. "Lemuel Snodgrass."

"William Jennings Bryan." The hobo chuckled again as if he'd said something funny. "Pleased to make your acquaintance."

I nodded.

"Best be quiet as mice." He put a dirty finger to his lips. "We can have a heart-to-heart once the train is in motion."

I watched as he pulled a plug of tobacco from his coat pocket, cut a piece off with a pocket knife, and, popping it into his mouth, began working his jaws with a small sigh of pleasure.

We watched each other until the light from the crack grew almost too dim to see by, and then the hobo closed his eyes, and I did too.

When I woke up, the day had settled into dusk. Sounds carry in the evening, and I could hear the workers back at their platform chores. Soon they were loading the other half of the freight car. It seemed to take them another hour, and then I heard the rumbling of the door as they pulled it closed and the sound of a metal latch locking it.

I could sense the hobo watching me as I got up and made my way over, close to the piece of board that was broken. When I pressed an eye up to the crack, I could see that most everything had been cleared from the platform. It looked like those who had been dining at the restaurant were gathered outside the station with their bags. In the illumination of the overhead electric lights, I could make out the golden-red hair of the strawberry blonde. I could hear her laughing at something the fat man was saying. By squinting in another direction, I noticed a figure on horseback at the other end of the platform. It was Albert.

What was he waiting for?

Then I heard it—the whistle of a train. It must be a freight coming through. Albert would be watching for anyone making an attempt to run from hiding and hop aboard a freight car.

In a few minutes a locomotive chuffed its way up to the station and came to a stop with a great complaining of metal and an exhalation of steam. My view of the station was blocked by the engine and the cars behind it, but I stayed where I was. It was good to stand after sitting in a cramped position for so long. Over the next while, the train seemed to shunt back and forth, and then, with a huge shudder, the car I was in lurched forward, sending me sprawling onto something wooden and sharp.

I hollered from the pain, but I don't think anyone heard me.

The freight had been coupled to the cars on the siding, and we moved out of Jackson Junction. Picking myself up, I caught a glimpse through the crack of Albert riding alongside, watching. And I thought I saw my carpet bag hooked onto the side of his saddle. I mourned its loss, not just for my change of clothes and my drawing portfolio but for the few mementoes I had left of Ma and Pa. Now all I had was Pa's watch, which I kept handy in one of my jacket pockets, and the neckerchief I wore with my initials embroidered by Ma.

With the train picking up speed, I eased myself back to the niche where I'd been sitting between piles of canvas. It was pitch black in the car now, but I could hear the hobo's breathing.

"With all this canvas, we should be able to make ourselves something of a bed for the night," he muttered, and I heard him working his pocket knife on a piece of rope and freeing some folds of the tent material. "There, a blanket for you and one for me. The luxuries of rail travel!"

I was grateful to have a length of canvas at my disposal and was able to make it into something of a nest in the small space that I had. I could feel my feet against the hobo's canvas-covered body.

"Thank you, William . . . er . . . Jennings . . ."

"I was just joshin' you, kid. Call me Zach. That's almost my real name. Care to tell old Zach here where you're headed to?"

"It's more I'm headed 'away from' rather than 'headed to,'" I said.

"On the run?"

As the freight sped rhythmically over the rails, I found myself giving Zach a full account of the events that had brought me to the point of hiding out in the back of a freight car.

Zach told me his own story. In his heyday he had been a prospector in Montana and then in the Klondike with some good returns for his efforts, but his profits were regularly depleted by liquor and gambling.

"Stud poker and demon rum have had their evil way with me," he sighed. "Take my advice, Lemuel, resist the bottle and the fifty-two-card pack."

Gradually we became talked out and I could feel myself nodding off.

"G'night, Zach," I said, through a yawn.

"Good night, boy." I could hear him rustling the canvas into a more comfortable position.

In the night, the train stopped at a couple of stations, but I had no trouble drifting back to sleep. When daylight seeped into the car through the broken board, I roused myself.

"Where do you think we're headed?" I asked Zach as he shared some stale bread and cheese with me from his hobo pack.

"Don't rightly know." Zach picked a piece of cheese from one of the gaps among his teeth. "Being a Chautauqua, they have to run this tent past six or seven towns that they've already set tents up in."

"Cripers—that's a lot of tents."

"You got that," Zach said. "It's a big outfit. I went out with a girl who played a piccolo in an all-female band—must be about fifteen years back. The band would play one night at one Chautauqua and then catch a train to play the next night in the next town on the circuit." Zach cut himself a plug of tobacco for dessert, offering me a chew, but I declined.

"Elvira," he said as he settled into chewing.

I gave him a quizzical look.

"That was her name. The piccolo player. We parted ways when I lost all my worldly belongings in a poker game."

I figured we'd finally reached our destination when our car was manoeuvered onto a siding. I hadn't really thought about what I might do once the train arrived. Would it be better to stay hidden until the cars were being unloaded and look for an opportunity to slip out and make a run for it? Or should I post myself right by the door, ready to leap out once it was opened? This seemed to be what Zach had in mind. He was at one side of the door, limbering up his legs.

"Hit the ground running," Zach said as I positioned myself at the other side of the door. "And don't head the same direction as me. If there's a yardman watching, it's best to be split up. Run like the bejeebers, that's my motto."

As I waited, I plunged a hand into my jacket pocket to check on my money. The wad of bills was not there.

"Hey!" I shouted.

Madly, I checked the other pocket and was relieved to feel the envelopes with the coins. My fingers searched for the bills.

Gone.

I looked over at Zach. It was dim enough in the car that I couldn't see much of him, but I knew he was bracing himself for any attempt I might make to retrieve the money he had picked from my pocket.

"Why, you—" I leaped at him, but as I did, the car door rolled open. My hands only managed to brush Zach's jacket as he jumped to the ground. True to his motto, he hit the ground running and ran like the bejeebers. I flung myself after him. For a brief second, I registered the surprised expression on the face of the young man who'd opened the door. But as I jumped, my foot caught on a coil of rope, and I went plummeting headfirst into the gravel alongside the main track. Instinctively I put out a hand to break my fall and to keep my face from becoming a human gravel scoop. My left hand ploughed through the small rocks and sharp pebbles, and I felt a wrenching pain shoot along my arm from my wrist. It was so sharp that I cried out, the kind of noise I'd heard from a dog yelping when it's on the losing end of a dogfight.

After a couple of seconds the pain ebbed, but when I rolled over, it struck me again. I closed my eyes and choked back a sob. When I opened them, I found myself staring up into the face of the girl with the strawberry blonde hair—the same face I'd noticed in the Harvey House, except that now her eyes were obscured by dark glasses.

"Welcome to Paradise," she said.

CHAPTER 7

Paradise, I was soon to discover, was the name of the town where the Chautauqua was setting up for its next show. My nosedive into the gravel was witnessed by a fair crowd of the town's inhabitants, mainly children, who had gathered out of curiosity to see the unloading of the tent and props. The crowd had obligingly parted to make way for Zach's escape with my money in his pocket.

The girl with the strawberry blonde hair kneeled down beside me. "Are you going to be okay?"

I started to say something but then blacked out. I felt a splash of water hit my face. The fat man who had presided over the table at the restaurant yesterday was bending over me.

"Riding the rails," he said. "A hazardous profession. Were it not for the fact that I, too, in my younger years had occasion to navigate the steel highway through the means of borrowed accommodation, I should be summoning the authorities. Seeing, though, that you have sustained an injury, I prefer to put myself into the shoes, or shall we say the sandals, of the Samaritan at the wayside, and we shall instead dress your wounds."

Even with the pain shooting through my lower arm, I was able to figure out that the fat man enjoyed the sound of his own voice and knew how to wrap plain speech up in a quilt of extra words.

"Raymond," he called out to the man who had opened the freight car door, "give this youngster an assisting hand and get him across the street to the hotel. Are you able to stand, son?"

I tried to stand up but in the process wrenched my hurt arm and collapsed again.

"You'd better carry him, Raymond. And Robert, you'd best go along. See if you can determine whether or not we need summon a real practitioner of the medical arts." The fat man gave me a nod. "Robert—Mr. Tremain—while not certified, has the fingers of a healer, I'm told. We shall trust to his digital expertise."

"Sure thing, Uncle Ambrose. I can rehearse Doctor Cyrus Sawbones while I check him over." Tremain was something of a dandy, wearing a silk tie and a checkered suit.

"You do that," the fat man chuckled. "It's your best skit, but I expect you will continue to find ways in which to embellish it."

Raymond didn't have any trouble hefting me into his arms. A few kids followed us, parading behind the man in the checkered suit and the strawberry blonde. Looking up, I could see a large banner strung across the street announcing the Chautauqua and the dates of the shows.

Eased onto a divan in the parlour of the Paradise Hotel, I relaxed and tested my hurt arm. Robert Tremain removed his suit coat, rubbed his hands together, flexed his fingers and cracked his knuckles in the process.

"Nurse Thundermug." He nodded to the girl. "Prepare for perjury . . . er, surgery . . . vat I mean to say is sharpen up the sawblade . . ." He rattled on.

Tremain carefully felt my arm, moving it slightly this way and that. But I couldn't help hollering out when he pressed my wrist.

"Sprained, I believe," he said, abandoning Dr. Sawbones' voice. "Round up a good-sized bandage and something we can use for a sling, Maggie. Ask the housekeeper. No bones broken. You should live to ride the rails again." Robert Tremain winked at me.

In a few minutes Maggie returned with a rolled bandage, what looked like a ripped-apart flour sack, a basin of cold water and a washcloth.

"Very good, Nurse Thundermug." Although Robert Tremain had slipped back into his Dr. Sawbones voice, he was very careful binding up my wrist, fashioning a sling, and then getting my arm into it. Even so, I could feel beads of sweat breaking out on my brow.

"What's your name?" the girl asked, and then she blushed. "I didn't mean to be rude. I'm Maggie Tremain—I'm the junior girl with the Chautauqua." She removed her dark glasses. Her eyes were the deep blue of larkspur blossoms.

"Leroy," I said. "Leroy Barnstable."

Maggie pressed the cool cloth to my forehead. "But my friends call me Doodlebug." I realized that no one had called me by my nickname since Ma and I had left Carrington well over a year ago. It felt strange and alien as I said it.

"Doodlebug!" Maggie had a laugh that was pretty close to music.

I felt a blush coming to my cheeks.

"Nurse T.," Robert Tremain said, putting on his checkered coat and straightening his collar and tie in the mirror hanging over the fireplace in the parlour, "I shall leave Master Doodlebug in your capable hands. I'll be with Uncle Ambrose in a meeting with some of the good citizens of Paradise while the tent is being set up."

"Thank you, Mr. Tremain." My voice didn't come out very loud, but I think he heard me. He wiggled his fingers in a small backward wave as he headed to the front door.

"Doodlebug?" Maggie asked.

"I like to draw," I said. "My pa said he was pretty sure I was born with a pencil in my hand. Then he would say 'it was a mighty difficult birth for your ma.'"

Maggie laughed. "It staggers the imagination."

She had a way of putting her hand to her mouth when she smiled, and I felt like reaching up and moving it away from her lips. They were too beautiful to conceal.

"Are you and Mr. Tremain related?" I asked her.

"Yes—slightly." Maggie pressed a fresh wet cloth to my forehead. "He's my father." She gave me another of her smiles. "We've just begun the Chautauqua circuit for the summer. I work in the children's tent, and Dad does character impressions."

Maggie smoothed the collar on her dress. It had daisies stitched on it and made me think of the girls at school chanting "loves me, loves me not."

"But tell me, why were you stowing away in our freight car?"

I didn't say anything for a minute. Just closed my eyes. After what Zach had done to me, I figured it was better to tell too little than too much.

"My ma died a while back, and I thought it was time to get out and find a job." I reached up to touch the cloth on my forehead and encountered Maggie's fingers. A thrill ran through my body. "I was stowing away because I didn't have much money, and that hobo who took off when the train stopped made off with pretty much all I had."

"If we'd only known, someone could have chased him. Scotty's a good runner."

"Scotty?"

Maggie blushed. "He's one of the tent boys," she said. "College kids who take on summer jobs working for Chautauqua—you know, raising the tents when we go into a new town, taking them down and packing them up when we're ready to leave."

"The guy who carried me over?"

"No, that was Raymond. He's another one of the crew."

Just then the hotel door banged open as two men struggled to bring in a large trunk.

"You want this upstairs?" A tall handsome guy with the kind of college haircut and square jaw you'd see in magazine shirt ads had hold of one of the trunk handles. He paused and grinned at Maggie, but the tent boy at the other end rammed him and said, "Keep moving, Scotty."

"Scotty." Maggie's eyes followed them as they struggled up the stairs. "And Orville. They've been with Chautauqua the last couple of years. I'll ask Uncle Ambrose if you can bunk in with them for a few days—at least until your arm is better."

"That's awfully kind of you." Morning sunlight streamed through the parlour window, making her hair look like spun gold. "Tell me about Chautauqua," I said.

"What do you want to know?" Maggie leaned back at the far end of the sofa and folded her hands in her lap.

"Everything. Carrington was too small for the Chautauqua. Ma and Pa told me they took me with them to see it in Spirit Rapids, but I was only two years old. Pa was still telling Billy Tubb's jokes ten years later, and Ma used to rave about Adeline Scotti singing opera."

"Chautauqua." Maggie said the word slowly as if there were magic in it and she didn't want to spill any of it. "It's a stage that can suddenly appear in the middle of the prairie, in places where there's been nothing more going on than the ladies' sewing club or a Sunday sermon or an amateur hour at the local high school. A stage with footlights and spotlights in front of a sea of people on folding chairs and benches, all under the canvas roof of a huge tent. There are musicians, actors and actresses, singers, famous lecturers, comedians, magicians. Six days and nights of shows, each day different. Most people can't wait for the Chautauqua to come to town."

"You love it, don't you?"

"Daddy and Uncle Ambrose have been on the stage, well, practically forever. Doing Lyceum programs in the winter, working Chautauqua circuits in the summer."

"Lyceum?"

"The Chautauqua developed from them. Lectures, music, dramatic shows. Most of the big cities have Lyceum stages."

"I've never been to a big city."

"My mama was a pianist at the theatres. Until she got sick."

"Is she—?"

"She died seven years ago, when I was ten." There was a tremble in Maggie's voice, like a leaf stirred by a spring breeze.

"Oh . . . I'm sorry."

"But you're more an orphan than I am, aren't you? You've lost your pa too."

"Yeah, a little over a year ago. I'm coming up seventeen." I didn't want her to know that was still nine months away.

I spilled out the whole story of Pa's accident and everything that had led to us moving to Cutter's Creek.

Maggie took my good hand and gave it a squeeze when I was finished. Her touch sent a shiver through me.

"I'm sorry, I have to go," she said. "It's time to put medicine in my eyes. I nearly lost my eyesight a while back. I won't be long."

Ambrose Poindexter returned from his meeting just as Maggie came back. She pleaded my case, and I watched him put his arm around her and give her a little hug.

"Of course, my dear," he said. " Our canvas abode can, I am certain, accommodate a stray for a few days. My boy," he said, turning to me, "allow me to offer you the hospitality of players on the road. Rusticity—but good company. Our door, or more correctly, our tent flap, is open to you."

Just then Maggie's father strolled in. "Ah . . . Nurse T." He gave her a grave nod, but I noticed a mischievous twitch at the corner of his mouth. "I see you have revived the spirits of this young man." Then he turned to me. "How's the wrist?"

"Er . . . I think it's better, sir. The sling really helps."

"But here it is noon already! Won't you join us for a bite to eat, Mr.—?" He looked at me questioningly.

"Barnstable, Leroy Barnstable."

"Well, Mr. Barnstable, as they say, 'Starve a fever, feed a sprain.'"

I was famished, and I noticed that both Maggie and her father watched with some amusement as I devoured three sandwiches and two bowls of soup to their single portions—and still had room for a huge piece of coconut cream pie. But Ambrose Poindexter seemed to notice nothing extraordinary in my appetite and managed to eat as much as I did.

When we finished, the men excused themselves to smoke on the verandah while Maggie and I stayed at the table, sipping our glasses of lemonade.

"I've been thinking about your drawing," Maggie said, massaging her eyes. "You might help—"

"Sure. What would you like me to do?"

"Depends on what you can draw."

"Almost anything. Quickest draw in the west." I gave her a grin.

"I can't draw a straight line to save my soul." Maggie put her glasses back on and shook her head.

"Straight lines—hugely overrated. Curvy ones are much more interesting."

"Is it your drawing hand you've hurt?"

"No—I'm not a southpaw."

"I'm thinking you could really give me a hand with the junior program. You know—helping us with details for costumes, maybe just sketching a bit for one group while I'm working with another?"

"Sounds like fun." I flexed the fingers on my good hand.

CHAPTER 8

Maggie walked me over to a baseball field where the Chautauqua tent had been erected. It was as big as the circus tent in Spirit Rapids, but the canvas was brown. Maggie told me that all the Chautauqua tents were brown so that no one would confuse the shows with a travelling circus. Small triangular flags fluttered from the poles that served as tent supports. Beyond the baseball field I glimpsed a lake.

"That smaller tent . . ." Maggie pointed to what looked like a baby elephant to the mammoth. "That's mine."

"Yours?"

"For the juvenile program. The town kids will be waiting to find out what's going to happen for the week."

When we arrived, there were two dozen children outside the entrance.

"Hey, everyone!" Maggie clapped her hands and the shrieking and chattering died down. "Welcome to this year's Chautauqua. I'm Miss Tremain and I'm in charge of everything for you young people."

Most of the kids would be able to count their years on the

fingers of two hands, but there were a few that would need to use some toes as well.

"We're going to have a great time over the next few days. There will be shows for you to see in the morning, and then in the afternoon we'll be setting up a king's court. I wonder who will be king? And queen?"

Maggie's question was met with a chorus of little ones calling out, "Me. Me. I wanna be queen! King!"

"Well, we won't choose until tomorrow. We'll have crafts in the afternoon, and we'll practise a play for the pageant on the final day. And, of course, there will be stories and songs . . ."

"Who's he?" A boy with a mop of red hair and a face that was more freckles than not, pointed a finger at me.

"Why, that's Mr. Doodlebug." Maggie laughed and several of the kids joined in. "He's our artist extraordinaire. If we need a mask, a king's crown or a treasure map—you name it—Mr. Doodlebug will make it."

"How'd he get a broken arm?" a little girl with ringlets and a huge bow in her hair asked.

"Mr. Doodlebug?" Maggie raised her eyebrows, and I knew she wanted me to answer this one myself.

"What? This?" I used my good arm to point at the sling. "Last town I was in, see, there was this mighty wind came along—a whirlwind near as gusty as a tornado. It swept me right up in the air. Which is a mighty odd feeling. I was sailing across the sky, looking down at cows munching away in meadows, and kids hurrying home from a swimming hole, and moms in their backyards unpegging their washing from clotheslines. It seemed like I was going to stay up there forever. But then, wouldn't you know it, that wind began to get tired, and as quick as it had picked me up, it dropped me down again."

Maggie gave me a look over the tops of her glasses, her eyes wide, an amused smile on her face.

"And when it did, it plunked me down right on top of an old billy goat who took an instant dislike to someone landing on him like that, and before I could get up proper and get my balance, he butted me in my left arm and near broke it in two."

The eyes of the smaller children had turned into circles of amazement. I heard a hushed "gee whillikers" and a "gosh almighty," but the older ones gave me the kinds of snorts you'd expect to get for telling a real whopper.

"I think we can use you during the story hour too," Maggie said.

In a minute she had all the children gathered around her, and they were excitedly telling her about how they were decorating their bicycles for the Chautauqua parade the following morning.

"You'll be parading through town to the Chautauqua grounds. Then you'll come here to the junior tent for the morning program." She beamed a smile at them.

When the children were gone, Maggie waved to Scotty, beckoning him to follow us inside the tent.

"Scotty," she said, "this is Leroy."

"Call me Doodle."

Scotty raised an eyebrow. "Hey, kid." He flashed a set of perfect teeth at me. "That was quite the pratfall you took this morning." Then he turned to Maggie. "You need any help getting things set up for tomorrow? I left Raymond and Orville putting up the fence—they don't really need me. Is where we put the piano okay?"

I drifted over to the side of the tent and listened as Maggie told Scotty where she wanted the trestle tables and chairs set up. Then Maggie paused, looking over at the back of the stage.

"Do you think you could paint a backdrop, Doodle? Maybe a castle."

"Sure."

"Here's a big roll of building paper. Scotty, fix up a couple of wooden crosspieces so we can tack the backdrop to them."

While Scotty hammered away, I sketched a turreted fairy tale castle with a drawbridge, a moat and woods in behind it.

"That's wonderful," Maggie said. Then she uncapped some bottles of tempera. "It's perfect for King Arthur's court and for the fairy tales I'll be telling the little ones. *Cinderella. Sleeping Beauty.* Don't you think it's marvellous, Scotty?"

Scotty grunted.

"And thanks for your help. We've kept you long enough. When we're finished painting, I'll send Doodle over to your tent. Uncle Ambrose said it would be fine if he bunked with you guys for awhile."

Maggie smiled, but I sensed Scotty wasn't as happy about everything as she was.

Maggie handed me a handful of paintbrushes, and we began painting the backdrop. I busied myself with the castle, while she worked green tempera into the treetops.

When we finished the backdrop, both of us were tired and hungry.

"That's great!" Maggie said, plunking herself down on the piano stool. As she rinsed out our paintbrushes, she looked up at me and smiled. "You're a sweetheart."

"So are you," I said, blushing.

"I bet the Anvil Chorus has got supper started."

"The Anvil Chorus?"

"The tent boys—Raymond and Orville and Scotty. That's what we call them sometimes, because they're so busy pounding steel pegs with hammers."

Maggie took me over to the crew tent.

When we got there, Raymond was busy stirring a pot on a camp stove.

"Hey, kid, how's the arm? It's my turn to cook tonight. Almost too hot to eat, isn't it? But setting-up day always gives me an appetite. Poindexter says you'll be batchin' and bunkin' with us— so welcome. We won't put you on mess duty right away. Wait till your arm gets better."

"Where are your partners in crime?" Maggie asked.

"Your Uncle Ambrose asked them to go downtown to check the posters on the billboards for the first-day program."

"Whatever you've got in the pot smells very tempting." Maggie laughed. "But I'd better get back to the hotel before they send out a posse for me."

Raymond stopped stirring the stew for a minute, and we watched her walk all the way across the baseball field. Maggie was the kind of person you couldn't help watching.

"You see a lot of pretty girls working the Chautauqua but next to Clementine Cavallero herself, I gotta say that Maggie Tremain is somethin' to set your eyes on. Pity she has to wear those glasses all the time."

In a matter of minutes, Orville and Scotty came into the tent. Scotty was carrying a cardboard container of ice cream.

"Eat fast," he said. "This walnut ripple isn't going to stay hard very long in this heat."

I had no trouble tearing into the stew Raymond had put together, sopping up the gravy with slices of homemade bread that one of the sponsors' wives had brought by.

When we'd finished our ice cream, Raymond lit up his pipe and the other boys sipped cups of tea.

"Come with me, sport," Orville said, tapping me on the shoulder as I began to nod off. "You've had a long day, and you're working the junior tent tomorrow. So you'll need your shut-eye. A bunch of little kids can wear you out faster than a ball game that's gone into extra innings."

They'd set up a cot for me next to theirs, and I don't think I'd ever seen anything so welcome in my life. Orville helped me get my shirt off and then redid my sling. I stripped down to my skivvies, put aside the blanket and pulled the sheet over me.

Despite the murmur of the boys talking in the background, the clink of dishes being washed and the regular chorus of frogs croaking from the lake at the edge of the woods, I expected I'd be asleep faster than you could say "Parade in the morning at nine." But when I closed my eyes, I was haunted by the face of Albert and could feel his rage.

I forced myself to think of other things. The train ride. Robert Tremain acting like a demented doctor. And Maggie in the parlour—the way those coppery curls framed her heart-shaped face, the deep blue of her eyes when she took her glasses off, her full lips the colour of wild rose petals.

But it wasn't Maggie's voice I heard as I finally drifted off to sleep. It was Ma whispering, "Sweet dreams."

CHAPTER 9

"Rise and shine, Doodle! Poindexter wants everyone out for the parade," Orville shouted, banging a porridge pot.

Scotty was frying some bacon on the camp stove.

My sling had come off in the night, but my wrist was feeling a lot better so I didn't bother putting it back on. Scotty plunked a plate of bacon and eggs and a steaming cup of tea in front of me.

"Are we going to be parading on foot?" I asked.

"Some of us." Orville chased a bit of egg yolk around his plate with a piece of last night's homemade bread. "But Poindexter, Maggie and the musicians will parade with the town boosters in their cars."

When we got to the end of Main Street that was farthest from the Chautauqua grounds, I was wishing I had a better suit of clothes. My jacket was rumpled and my shirt was dirty with a few blood spots showing from where my hand had bled from the gravel cuts. I did have on my best trousers when I took off from Cutter's Creek, but with all the growing I'd been doing in the last few months, the pant bottoms hovered just flush with my ankles, and I hadn't managed to get all the dried mud off them—or my socks and boots.

I spotted Ambrose Poindexter taking up the back seat of a touring car, its top down. He had his pork-pie hat in one hand and was waving to everyone even though the parade hadn't begun to move. Signs slung on the sides and back of the car announced PARADISE CHAUTAUQUA—JUNE 4–9—DON'T MISS IT!

Maggie waved at me before climbing into another car with her dad. She was wearing a white dress with a sailor collar and a wide-brimmed sun hat that made a perfect frame for her face as she looked back at me and the tent boys.

Raymond, Scotty and Orville had gotten out of their work clothes and were in their best duds too.

"Wow! There she is!" Orville made an appreciative whistle.

All three of them were looking at a beautiful, dark-haired woman sitting in the back seat of a shiny touring car that had just pulled in. Her dress looked like it could have been made out of spun moonlight. She had taken her hat off and was using it to fan herself. The day had already pulled up yesterday's muggy heat like a heavy blanket.

"Clementine Cavallero," Orville whispered, a touch of awe in his voice.

"Who's she?" I asked.

"She's Cleopatra and Heloise and Juliet all at once," said Raymond, who'd told me he was studying the classics and English literature at college.

"She's an opera singer." Scotty's gaze was still fixed on her. "She'll be performing this evening, and I'm going to be ducking into the tent tonight to catch that one."

"Opera I can live without." Orville adjusted his collar and mopped his brow with his pocket handkerchief. "But I'm not going to miss seeing her on stage the way I did in Jackson Junction. She's a real knockout!"

"Yeah." Raymond sighed. "All those jewels . . ."

A cheer went up as the parade began to move. The cars led the way followed by a horse-drawn wagon draped in colourful bunting. It carried the Quarter Time Quintet, who were scheduled to play in the afternoon and evening shows. Their jaunty music set some of the children coming behind to skipping, and I felt my own toes itching to join them. Bicyclists had crepe-paper streamers woven into their wheel spokes, noisy with clackers. Car horns honked. Balloons floated from car door handles, bicycle handlebars and children's hands. People lining the street cheered. The tent boys were smiling non-stop and handing out flyers urging everyone to buy a pass to the shows. Raymond gave me some to hand out as well.

"Come to the Chautauqua. Don't miss it!" I said, pressing flyers into people's hands. "Six full days of shows. Great today but even better as the week goes on."

From the end of Main Street the parade wound its way over to the Chautauqua grounds. People began to stream into the tent for the morning program, and I spied Maggie heading for the junior tent.

"Oh, good." She gave me a smile as I got to the tent's entrance. "You can check the tickets while I get everyone settled inside. Make sure every kid has a ticket."

Some of the children recognized me from yesterday and called out, "Hey, Mr. Doodlebug," or even, "Hi, story guy."

The program was due to begin in half an hour, but most of the children were inside the tent in fifteen minutes. I could hear the excited buzz and chatter growing. A couple of the younger ones were shrieking and running around.

That's when Maggie struck a chord on the piano, and I heard her voice taming those inside. "While we're waiting, let's begin learning our Chautauqua song." Maggie beckoned to the tallest boy among the children. "Gordie, would you mind coming up here and using the pointer so everyone can follow along on the chart while I play the piano?"

Gordie beamed, enjoying the attention he was suddenly attracting.

Maggie played an introduction on the piano and then nodded her head for Gordie to begin pointing to the words on the chart as she began singing:

> *Underneath the tent top,*
> *When the sun is high,*
> *I can't keep from smiling*
> *And here's the reason why:*
> *Boys and girls together—*
> *We're happy all day long.*
> *So take my hand and sing out*
> *Our own Chautauqua song.*

At first the children's voices were tentative, and they had a bit of trouble keeping up with Gordie's pointer. But Maggie had a strong, clear voice that drew them together.

"All right, everyone!" she called out:

Chau—tau—qua, Chau—tau—qua—
We bring our best for you.
Chau—tau—qua, Chau—tau—qua—
With friendship fast and true.

After they'd sung the song through a couple of times, Maggie briefed the group again about what was in store for them throughout the week. Then she introduced the magician who was the star attraction for the morning show. Giving the stage over to the Great Bonzini with his black top hat and red-lined cloak, she made her way to the back of the tent and gave me a wink. The Junior Chautauqua was up and running.

The children were enthralled as the Great Bonzini pulled lengths of brightly coloured silk from their shirts or made bouquets of artificial flowers materialize out of thin air. He plucked coins from their ears and did amazing tricks with a deck of cards. Objects from children's pockets, hidden in boxes, magically reappeared out of his hat.

Scotty had slipped into the tent and was staring at Maggie, not the Great Bonzini. I smiled at him, but he didn't smile back.

The Great Bonzini finished his act with a flourish of bright objects: toy birds, pinwheels, paper flowers and tiny puzzles rained down on the audience—treats they would be allowed to keep. Maggie hurried back to the stage in the midst of the applause and uproar and thanked the magician. Then she settled the children down by teaching them a freeze-and-be-silent gesture that required them not to move a muscle for thirty seconds. When everyone was quiet, she launched into a story, pointing to the fairy tale castle we'd painted onto the backdrop.

"There was once a king and his beautiful queen who lived in

a castle at the edge of a great forest . . ." Maggie wasn't the Great Bonzini, but she had their rapt attention as she continued telling the tale of *Sleeping Beauty*.

When the morning program finished and it was time for lunch, I could see Maggie had an adoring group of fans vying to hold her hand as she ushered everyone out of the tent to join their families. People who had taken the day off were setting out picnic lunches by their vehicles or on the grass at the edge of the ball diamond closest to the woods where there was some shade.

"Miss Tremain. Miss Tremain," one little boy was chanting. He had hold of Maggie's skirt and along with two or three others, was trying to get her attention.

Maggie stopped and he began telling her a long, involved story about a toad he had for a pet.

She waved me on and I headed over to the crew tent to see what the tent boys were doing for lunch. I found them alongside it, surrounded by half a dozen young women urging sandwiches and lemonade and pieces of cake on them. Everyone was laughing and having a good time.

"Bertha . . ." Orville was trying to talk through a mouthful of food. "Thish ish the best tongue san'wich . . ."

Scotty was almost choking with laughter. "You like a bit of tongue, don'cha, Orv, old boy?"

Raymond caught my eye and shook his head as if the two were beyond hope. "Hey, Doodle," he called out. "Get over here. These beauties have formed an association for the prevention of the starvation of the canvas crew—that includes you."

One of the beauties, who was a bit more than pleasantly plump, dug into her lunch basket and extended a hefty devilled-egg sandwich to me.

"Heavenly days." She giggled. "I'd give my eye teeth to have natural curls like you got . . . er, Doodle."

"That your real name?" Her companion gave me a big, toothy smile and poured me a glass of lemonade.

"It's Doodlebug," I said, before acquainting myself with the sandwich. And after I washed that first bite down with a swig of lukewarm lemonade, I added, "My stage name, you understand."

I have to say the girls who came to that first day's Chautauqua brought enough food to nourish an entire threshing crew. I was making my way through a giant-sized piece of chocolate cake, trying to manage it with one hand—my other wrist was still sore—when I saw Maggie coming toward us. She looked bemused when one of the girls helped clean some of the chocolate icing off my face with a napkin.

Maggie greeted the tent boys and said hi to the girls. Then she turned to me. "When you're finished, can I ask you a favour?"

"Sure," I said, smiling at her.

She motioned for me to follow her back to the junior tent. "This afternoon we'll be setting up King Arthur's court. The kids will be making speeches and then voting on who should be king and queen. They'll be choosing their lords' and ladies' names—that kind of thing. That's fine for the older ones, but I was wondering if you could come up with something to amuse the six- and seven-year-olds. Maybe do some drawing for them, or get them busy with crayons and paper?"

"The Doodle is at your service, my lady." I bowed to her flamboyantly and wrenched my sprained wrist in the process. I couldn't help groaning.

"Don't kill yourself on my account." Maggie gave me a smile and patted my good arm. "Now I just have to remember where I stored the drawing paper, pencils and crayons."

I had been quick to say the Doodle would be at her service, but I wasn't at all certain what I might do to keep the little ones occupied. Then I got an idea and began setting paper out at a couple of trestle tables to one side.

To begin the afternoon program, Maggie had everyone sing the Chautauqua Youth song a couple of times, and then she divided the group, sending the little ones into the corner where the tables were set up.

I had the smaller kids gather at my feet while I sat on one of the folding chairs and spoke in a soft voice.

"Today, while the big kids are choosing kings and queens and knights and ladies, we're going to be doing something even better."

"What?" one little boy asked.

"Castles. Every one of you will be designing your own castle. You can give it as many towers as you want, and you can put a big door or window in it. And do you want to know what will be inside that big door or window?"

"What?" they chorused.

"Why, you just whisper in my ear and give me a few minutes and my magic crayon will find that special person or creature."

In no time at all they were labouring over their crayoned drawings of castles.

"I got my window done," Myrtle Mae, a little girl in a dress with red polka dots and a bright red ribbon in her hair, shouted out, causing the group of older kids to pause and look our way.

"Shhh." I put a finger to my lips. "Come here, Myrtle Mae. Whisper in my ear what's just behind that window."

"A dragon," she said, speaking so softly I could hardly hear her.

"What does it look like?" I whispered back.

She watched, barely able to contain her excitement as I outlined a dragon with huge teeth and smoke coming out of its nostrils, according to her specifications.

"And polka dots," she informed me, casting an eye down at her own dress.

The whole group had stopped drawing their castles for a few minutes and gathered around Myrtle Mae while I completed the sketch. When they saw the results, there was a ripple of chatter: "Wow, that's good!" "You're an artist!" "I want a dragon too."

All at once, they were back in their places, working furiously on their own castles. From the stage, Maggie gave me a quick glance of approval as she was getting King Arthur's court into partners to practise their speeches.

After that I didn't have time to look around, I was so busy drawing princesses and kings and fairies, a couple of giants and quite a few more dragons.

We were just finishing up and Maggie was getting ready to bring the group back together as a whole, when a man poked his head into the tent. He looked around and signalled to Maggie that he wanted to speak with her. She told King Arthur's court to continue practising for a minute and went over to him. As he stepped inside, everyone went silent and stared.

"I'm Sheriff Earl. We were told there might be a runaway boy hiding out hereabouts."

My crayon, which was busy putting a long beard on a wizard in Jimmy's castle window, wobbled.

"Haven't seen anyone." Maggie smiled sweetly at him. "There's just our Chautauqua artist and myself and the children. Do you think one of these children might be who you're looking for?"

The man took off his hat and squinted at the children up by the stage and then at the smaller ones—most of them with crayons in their hands, a couple of them chewing on them. I bent over my drawing of the wizard.

"Nope. Don't seem likely," I heard the man say. "But if you see anyone suspicious, I'd appreciate it if you'd take a minute and drop in to the sheriff's office."

"Sure thing."

From the corner of my eye, I could see that Maggie had manoeuvered herself around so she was blocking the sheriff's view of me. "Do you know what the boy looks like?"

"No, not much of a description. And we wouldn't be worryin' that much about a kid takin' off in the summer to stretch his legs a bit. But we got a notification saying this one's been involved in horse-thieving and robbery."

"Robbery. My goodness, I'm glad you told me. I'll watch my . . ." I could sense Maggie struggling to think of something she needed to watch. "My belongings," she managed. Then she made a quick turn, clapped her hands and told all the children to gather in seats by the stage.

It wasn't until the last of the children had straggled away at the end of the afternoon and we were putting away crayons and paper that Maggie spoke to me about the sheriff's visit.

"Horse-thievery? Robbery?" She'd taken off her glasses and was looking at me with real concern in her eyes—those blue eyes that

I felt I could slip and fall into as easily as a swimming hole on the hottest day of summer.

And so I spilled out the rest of my story—all that had happened to me after coming to Cutter's Creek. I told her about borrowing Polish for the ride into Jackson Junction and that the money I'd taken was only half of what belonged to me.

"Albert or Virgil must have got the sheriff in Jackson Junction to send out a notice."

"But if he got his horse back—why?" Maggie moved closer to me and put her hand gently on my good arm, like a whisper.

"You'd have to know Albert and Virgil. They knew they owed me that money, but for me to take it—that's something they'd never forgive." My voice choked as Maggie's fingers give my arm a squeeze. "Your dad and your uncle—they won't want me to stay."

"It's okay," she said. "It'll be our secret."

CHAPTER 10

*T*here was no evening program in the junior tent so I joined Scotty, Orville and Raymond to watch the performances in the big tent. The tent boys muttered about having to stay at the back if they wanted to watch, but standing there in my rumpled and stained clothing, I was thankful to be behind everyone.

"We'll need a telescope to see her," Orville complained.

There was a sea of people on folding chairs and backless benches, people from Paradise—but also those who'd driven over from nearby smaller towns and farmers from the surrounding countryside.

I could feel a hum of excitement as people chatted and fanned themselves against the heat with programs.

Just below the stage, the Chautauqua musicians began to play. The buzz of talking settled into a quiet expectation as spotlights played against the stage curtain. The music was sweet, drifting out over the audience, and I recognized the song as one Ma used to play on her pump organ. The violin caressed the tune in a way that I knew would have brought tears to her eyes.

When the overture was finished, unseen hands parted the

curtain and pulled it to the sides. Volunteer kids from the high school were acting as stagehands, and I noticed two boys hovering at the edges. Then Ambrose Poindexter stepped into the spotlight at the centre of the stage.

"My dear friends of Paradise and those of you who have come from beyond Paradise, I join the Chautauqua performers and crew in welcoming you to the opening day of our week-long extravaganza of entertainment and educational enlightenment that we have been preparing for you over the course of many months." He had a voice that carried powerfully to the very back of the tent. "Now it may be presumptuous for us to feel that we can bring anything special to the gates of Paradise . . ." A small wave of laughter rippled through the audience. " But tonight we have—how can I put it in any other words?—an angel, whose voice has drawn envy and acclaim from around the world, the divine Clementine Cavallero . . ." The name drew spontaneous applause.

Ambrose Poindexter was on a roll. He expounded on the virtues of the other acts of the evening and then launched into a plea for the businessmen and professionals of Paradise to sign on as sponsors to ensure that the Chautauqua would be playing in their town again the next summer. I looked around to see if I could spot Maggie. It took a bit of time, but I finally picked out what I was pretty sure was the back of her head. She was seated close to the front.

When Maggie's uncle finally bowed off, the Quarter Time Quintet came onstage in their bright striped jackets and boater hats. Their brass instruments gleamed under the spotlights. They played a medley of marches and dance tunes that was certain to wake up anyone who might have drifted off during Ambrose

Poindexter's wordy introduction. A couple of the little girls, who had drawn castles for me earlier, were dancing their own little dances to the catchy music before a couple of the stagehands managed to get them back into their seats.

The Quarter Time Quintet was followed by Maggie's dad, who had abandoned his checkered suit and was doing a monologue as Dr. Sawbones in a beard and the rumpled attire of a country doctor. He had a bag out of which spilled a handsaw, a meat grinder and a length of rubber tubing.

"Vat's that you say, Nurse Thundermug? The patient has taken off? Taken off what? Oh—taken off running down the street. I thought you said he had a broken leg and couldn't valk . . ."

Raymond rolled his eyes. But the audience was roaring with laughter and clapping throughout the skit. I couldn't help chuckling too, but I tried not to laugh loud enough that the sophisticated college tent boys would notice.

After Tremain finished doing Dr. Sawbones, the Chautauqua musicians played a piece while he changed costume. When he came back onstage, he was dressed as an Indian with a full feather headdress that trailed down his back. I was expecting another funny routine, but he came up to the front of the stage, looking very serious.

Someone in the orchestra created a soft, rhythmic beat on a tom-tom, casting a spell over the audience.

"Great Manitou, hear me . . ." Tremain spoke in a deep, haunting voice. "I come to beg you, for my people, the people of the Great Plains, the people of the buffalo, to give us peace and let us live in the way our fathers lived . . ."

Maggie's father performed four monologues, and I was amazed at how he could slip from one personality into the next. Was this something that I might be able to do one day? It made my skin tingle just to think about it. And if I could make myself into someone totally different and people believed I was that person, wouldn't that be a perfect way to hide from the Grimbles of the world?

Ambrose Poindexter was back on stage. "And now, ladies and gentlemen, boys and girls, we are proud to present our main attraction of the evening, the world-renowned soprano who has sung for royalty and is here this evening to share her magnificent voice with those gathered . . ."

Somehow Maggie's uncle managed to make his introduction last the better part of a quarter of an hour as he slipped in yet another plea for the boosters in the town to commit pledges for the coming year.

When he was finished, the stagehands opened the curtains wide, and Clementine Cavallero stepped into the spotlight. The entire Chautauqua audience drew a breath . . . then there was a tremendous thunder of applause. In her raven black hair she wore a diamond tiara that picked up bits of light and sent it scattering throughout the tent. There were pendant jewels at her ears, and her low-cut gown allowed a full display of dazzling jewels in a choker and cascading necklace.

"Holy Toledo." Scotty gasped. "Will you look at that swag!"

"Forget the swag," Orville replied. "Look at that figure!"

"I'm lookin'," Raymond sighed.

And then Clementine Cavallero began to sing. It was opera music, and none of it was in English. But her voice cajoled, soared and swooped with shades of joy and sadness that made me feel faint. I couldn't imagine hearing anything more beautiful. After she finished each song, the tent erupted into applause.

Darkness seeped into the edges of the tent from the opened walls, and moths fluttered around the spotlights and floodlights as Clementine Cavallero was finishing her program.

"My dear people," she addressed the audience. "I have never felt more welcome. Thank you so very much. And now I will end with a favourite song of mine—one with words that will be familiar to all of you."

> *Mid pleasures and palaces, though we may roam,*
> *Be it ever so humble, there's no place like home!*
> *A charm from the skies seems to follow us there,*
> *Which, seek through the world, is ne'er met with elsewhere.*

I felt a lump in my throat as I thought about Pa and Ma, and the only home that had ever been a true home. Me at the kitchen table working on my sketches, brushing crumbs from cookies off the paper. Pa sitting back, enjoying an evening cup of coffee, dipping a gingersnap and madly trying to get it into his mouth before the dipped part fell off. Ma looking up from her mending and smiling at us. It was so long ago.

Clementine Cavallero now urged everyone to join in the chorus.

Home! Home! Her soprano tones rose over the swell of voices from the audience.

> *Sweet, sweet home!*
> *There's no place like home!*

The crowd drifted out of the tent into the warm evening toward waiting cars and wagons. Some carried sleeping children.

Older kids raced around getting the kinks out of their legs. Farmers chatted about late chores to be done as they went along. Townspeople ambled across the field to the sidewalks at the edge of the ballpark. Young lovers walked hand in hand. There was the noise of car motors catching and teams of horses being urged into motion with gee-ups and clicks of the tongue. Off in the distance a couple of dogs carried on a discussion with the rising moon.

I waited by the tent entrance for Maggie.

After the audience had gone, Clementine Cavallero emerged. She was linked arm in arm with Robert Tremain and had changed out of her opera finery. Even without her jewels and long gown, she looked like a queen. Maggie's father could well be her doting prince consort. In their wake, Maggie and her uncle followed.

"Hey, Doodle!" Maggie pulled away from the group and came over to me. "Wasn't that great? I could've listened to Clementine all night."

"Me too."

"I'm glad you waited. I wanted to tell you again what a great job you did with the little ones today. But would you believe it, my group was jealous and they want you to do something with them tomorrow. So I was thinking you could maybe help all the knights design a personal shield, and—for the ladies—they could decorate a cone-shaped hat."

"Your wish is my command."

For a minute, I could see she was giving my clothes a good going over, the way a gardener might look at a vegetable patch gone to weeds. She looked like she was going to say something about them but then changed her mind. In the dusk, I hoped she wouldn't be able to notice my cheeks burning. I still had the twelve dollars in coins that I'd taken from Virgil's dresser drawer and wondered if that would be enough to buy me a new outfit.

"Good night, Doodle." Maggie smiled and gave me a hug.

As she hurried away to catch up with her uncle, Orville took me aside.

"You've got yourself a little sweetie, don't you, Doodle, my boy?" he said, under his breath.

"Naw," I protested. "We were just talking about work."

"Well, you'd better watch out for Scotty." He nodded in his direction. "You know the song about 'My Little Margie'? Well, Scotty's been going around singing it, except he's changed the words to 'My Little Maggie.'"

Scotty was standing at the entrance to the crew tent with a scowl on his face. I looked away and couldn't think of anything to say.

It was a relief when Orville clapped me on the shoulder and said, "It's laundry night tonight." He was giving my clothes a once over. "Bath night too. How 'bout we head down to the lake for a plunge, and we'll take along a pail and some soap and scrub the duds a bit. I know my socks sure need a washin'."

When Raymond saw what we were up to, he grabbed some of his clothes too, and we all headed out past the woods to the lakeshore. The public beach was a mile farther down, but Orville found a spot close by where it was quite shallow near the shore. We began stripping down and I looked around, not too sure where to put the coins from my jacket pocket. Finally I decided to tuck them into the toe of my boot.

"Last one in's a rotten egg," Orville declared.

I was the rotten egg.

Past the horsetail reeds where the water was clear, Orville and Raymond were bobbing up and down. When I got near them, they began windmilling their arms and splashing me. I tried to retaliate, but it wasn't easy to do with just one arm.

We swam around or just floated for a while, enjoying the coolness of the water after the heat of the day. Orville went back to shore, got the bar of soap, and we took turns soaping ourselves before tackling our clothing. I was the only one who was washing everything I owned, and the guys helped me wring out my sorry wardrobe, then loaned me a towel to wear back to the tent. We hung our clothing on the ropes stretching out from the canvas to the pegs that secured the big tent.

"We'll need to take these off before the crowd arrives for the morning show." Orville eyed his underwear flying at half-mast.

I crawled into my bed and fell asleep before my head touched my pillow. I slept late too. When I finally woke up, strong morning light was seeping through the canvas, warming the interior. It looked like it would be another day in which we'd be rolling up the side panels to let air in. I inhaled the smell of the paraffin-treated canvas and the crushed grass of the ball diamond, and there was a lingering aroma of coffee and bacon even though the tent boys had disappeared somewhere. I was glad to spy a plate of bread and bacon they'd left out for me.

I wrapped my blanket around me and peeked out of the entrance to the crew's quarters, hoping no one would be nearby to see me collecting my laundry off the tent ropes.

In luck. The coast was clear, but the grass of the baseball diamond was wet. There were small pools of water surrounding first base and home plate. It had rained in the night, and I had been too sound asleep to notice. My clothing hung where I had left it, sopping wet. Orville and Raymond's socks and underwear were there too, but they had dry clothes to change into. Maybe they could loan me some of theirs.

I noticed one of the volunteer kids who worked as a stagehand wandering by.

"Where is everybody?" I asked him, pulling the blanket closer.

"I think everybody's down at the station picking up the new acts that've come in for today."

"I need you to do me a favour."

"Sure," he said. "Shoot."

"Go over to the junior tent. And if Maggie is there, tell her Doodle needs her right away."

I pictured myself doing the junior program naked as a jaybird!

CHAPTER 11

I must have looked a sight, all wrapped up in an Indian blanket, sitting on my cot. Maggie couldn't help laughing. She, of course, looked as crisp and fresh as a new-sprung buttercup, in a yellow dress with a pattern of wildflowers on it.

When I explained what had happened, she went over and felt my shirt.

"You're right. This is going to need a couple of hours in the sun to dry. We've got to get you into something right away." A smile brightened her face. "I know. I'll see what I can find in our costume box."

She was back in a few minutes, a pile of clothing in her arms. "You'd have to be a few sizes smaller to fit into King Arthur's costume, and besides, it's mainly cardboard and silver paper. But I found these at the bottom of a trunk. You can be either a tramp or a clown."

She dropped the clothes onto my cot. I looked at the mismatched pile of garments with some apprehension. On top lay a wrinkled clown suit with a couple of its big red buttons missing. Maggie must have read the dismay in my face.

"It's just for this morning—I know you can figure out something," she said. "I'll go and let you get dressed, but come over as soon as you can."

Spreading the garments out on my cot, I set aside a worn black dress jacket with a couple of calico patches stitched onto it and a pair of baggy trousers with more patches on the knees. I put on a collarless shirt that was more yellow than white and was thankful, in the absence of underwear, that it hung down to my knees. To keep the oversized trousers in place, I used a striped necktie as a belt. Unlike my own pants, which showed my ankles, these were too long, so I rolled up the bottoms. I stuck my right foot into my boot and quickly pulled it out again. I'd forgotten that I'd tucked my stash of coins into the toe last night. I shoved the coins into my pants pocket.

The tent boys had hung up a small mirror, and I borrowed Raymond's comb and hairbrush to try and tame my unruly curls before deciding that my tramp costume actually looked better with my hair in disarray.

If I'm going to be a tramp, I might as well go all the way.

I ran my fingers along a pan the boys had used to cook bacon and smudged the black that came off onto my cheeks and forehead. The hat for the clown suit had an artificial flower on it, and I borrowed it for the tramp's jacket lapel.

As I shuffled over to the junior tent, I wondered if Robert Tremain had got his start as a master of disguises in a similar way. I didn't have much time for such musing though. As soon as I came through the tent door, the little kids I'd worked with the day before flocked around me.

"Hey, Mr. Doodlebug!" Myrtle Mae giggled. "What are you?"

"How come you got on those funny clothes?" another piped up.

"Funny!" I pretended to be offended. "Zis wunnerful coat!" I patted the flower on my lapel. "Zees wunnerful pants!" I stretched out the baggy knees and did a kind of a curtsey. I'm not sure why my voice popped into the silly accent Pa used when he was telling jokes or goofing around on the way home from an auction—except it'd always made me chuckle, and right now a chuckle seemed kind of important.

The little ones shrieked with laughter, and Maggie was laughing too as she herded everyone into their seats to begin the morning program.

"Welcome, M'sieur Doodlebug," she said when they'd finished singing the Chautauqua song. "I'm glad you've found your proper clothes today."

"Yes." I bowed to the group. "Zis ees ze real me. I am—how do you say?—ze artist vagabond, but it took a day for my clozing to catch up wiz me!"

I decided to be a vagabond artist in a way that Robert Tremain would have done it—with unblinking conviction, living the role from the hairs on the top of my head to the tips of my toenails.

Once Maggie had the little kids off in their corner, I got to work getting the older boys tracing a shield outline onto large pieces of cardboard. Maggie had left out semicircular pieces for the ladies' coned hats.

"Now, zees you must design yourself, but I am 'ere to 'elp you wiz some of ze bits and pieces. Knights—you want lions on your shield? I shall draw you ze first one. Or a fleur-de-lys? Let me show you how eet ees done."

"How come you didn't have that accent yesterday?" Gordie, the kid who'd wielded the pointer for Maggie's song chart, gave me a bemused look.

"It comes wiz zee clothes," I informed him.

"Yeah." One of the girls gave him a gentle punch on the arm. "He's got a magic coat, don'cha know. Makes him talk funny."

They gathered around a spare piece of canvas Maggie had spread on the ground, anchored with some jars of tempera. A ten-year-old boy with cross-eyes and a catchy laugh asked me to sketch an eagle on his shield.

"Holy moley." He giggled when I was finished. "You *are* a magic artist."

Addie, who never missed an opportunity to remind the others that her dad, Paradise's pharmacist, was one of Chautauqua's sponsors, asked me to begin a curlicue design with roses in it for her hat. Once again, I was busier than a sheep farmer at shearing time. Every once in a while, though, I drew breath and glanced over at Maggie telling stories to the little ones.

Later that day I went downtown to a general store and came back with a full set of clothes.

The next day when I went over to the junior tent, I dressed up as the tramp again. Truth be told, I enjoyed being in costume and using a silly voice. Maggie liked it too and urged her uncle to come in and watch me one day. I could see he was pleased.

"My boy," he said, "I can see you have a natural inclination for performance. Nourish it with care and you will find yourself treading the hallowed boards that have known the footfall of Garrick, Booth and Barrymore. And, while you are momentarily at a loss for the physical necessities of food and shelter, bide with us. Yes, son, bide with us for as long as we have canvas to spread between yourself and the stars of night."

"Thank you, sir," I said. "It will be a pleasure."

As Poindexter left, Scotty came up and pulled me aside. "If you're going to be travelling with us you better start helping out more."

Scotty's mood didn't improve at all as the children from the junior tent paraded onstage for their closing-night pageant. And it only got worse when Maggie sang my praises to the congregation of proud parents in the main tent. As I went onstage in my tramp outfit to take a bow, she took my hand, and I saw Scotty storm out.

A travel lecturer was on next, and with the help of magic lantern slides he took the people of Paradise on a trip down the Amazon. He was an expert at imitating bird and animal calls. Children in the audience did a good deal of chirping and squawking with him.

Then the Palace Players performed *The Warden's Daughter*, a drama in three acts with a thrilling shootout between a villainous prisoner and the jailer.

When a group of Swiss bell-ringers—the only thing Swiss about them was their costumes—brought down the final curtain, the people of Paradise clapped thunderously. There were five encores. It was as if the audience didn't want to let go of this world of the big brown tent and all that had appeared before them on the stage.

"Thank you one and all! What a wonderful week! We're looking forward to entertaining you next year with an even more marvellous array of acts." Ambrose Poindexter smiled broadly, waving a handful of signed pledges.

As people filed away, I stripped off my tramp jacket and, in my shirtsleeves and patched costume trousers, helped the crew boys as best I could to dismantle the tent.

The show was over for the people of Paradise, but we would be loading the train cars and heading for the next town before the night was over. I had been with the Chautauqua for only a few days in Paradise when we did our closing show. But I felt like I'd been with the company forever, that all the grief of the last year and a half was a dim, distant past. Then all of a sudden a sharp pain in my sprained wrist brought back the spectres of Albert and Virgil, who were certainly still on my trail.

CHAPTER 12

Flausbech wasn't a whole lot different-looking than Paradise. The tent boys immediately dubbed it "Flyspeck," and it was a bit smaller than the town where we'd finished up last night. They were setting the tents up here in a park at the edge of town. Although my sprained wrist was pretty well recovered, I thought it would be folly to try and help Scotty, Raymond and Orville as they laced canvas together and heaved up the tent poles, pulled ropes taut and pounded in tent stakes with a sledge hammer.

At loose ends, with all the activity that was going on, I got into my new set of clothes and went in search of Maggie. It felt good to have dungarees that fit, and a crisp cotton shirt.

I knew Maggie, her father and her uncle were staying at a rooming house a couple of blocks off Flausbech's main street. There was no proper hotel, but the rooming house was huge with gables sprouting out of it from all sides and a couple of stairways going along the outside walls to second- and third-storey doors. The property was surrounded with a wrought-iron fence. I was tapping a rhythm against it with a cottonwood tree branch when I saw Maggie and her uncle emerge from the front door.

"Ah, Leroy, my boy." Ambrose Poindexter beckoned me over. "During that lengthy and, I might say rather sleepless train journey, I had—in my state of wakefulness—an opportunity to reflect on your particular skills with crayon and paper. We do, of course, desire that you continue to woo the youngsters with your talent. But it occurred to me that you might also enchant some of our adult patrons by setting up an easel just outside the gate. Sketch the likeness of those willing to part with twenty-five cents for a crayon portrait and you will have a means of garnering some remuneration for your own pockets. In addition, of course, it will attract interest to our ticket booth."

Maggie winked at me, and I knew she must have planted this idea in her uncle's mind.

"Wow," I said. "Do you really think I could do it?"

"My boy." Poindexter raised his walking stick slightly into the air. "One of the major tenets of the Chautauqua way of life is the promotion of positive thought. If you think you can do it—you can do it!"

Maggie and her uncle were off to charm Chautauqua's potential sponsors at a meeting in the town hall. Once they turned the corner and headed to Main Street, I raced back to the Chautauqua site. I took one of the easels used to present posters of the coming attractions and some crayons and paper from the junior tent and carried them over to where the tent boys were taking a lunch break. When I explained what Ambrose Poindexter had asked me to do, Raymond, who had finished his sandwich and was smoking his pipe, agreed to pose for me.

"Ten minutes," he declared between puffs. "That's all it takes a good crayon artist to do a portrait. One of my college chums spends his summers sketching at county fairs and exhibitions. He can do a decent likeness in eight minutes, but then he's had tons of practice."

I used a light blue crayon to sketch Raymond's square-cut face and block in his full wings of hair, combed back with a part in the middle. He had heavy eyebrows, a dominant lower lip and a cleft in his chin. I squinted at the blue outline. After making his ears a bit larger and widening the base of his nose, I grabbed a black crayon to darken the lines and work in the details. Then a bit of red on his cheeks and lips, brown for his eyes, some blue shading along the sides of the face, under the chin and around the eyes to suggest depth. I used the edge of the black crayon to shade the stubble along the lower part of his face. The Anvil Chorus hadn't had time to shave this morning.

"Twelve and a half minutes," Orville announced, with his pocket watch in his hand.

"Hey, Doodle. Not bad at all," Raymond said.

"A whiz kid," Scotty said, with a touch of sarcasm. "I suppose you can sing like Caruso and dance like Nijinsky too."

Raymond reached into his pocket and pulled out a quarter.

"Naw." I shook my head. "You guys have been—"

"Take it, kid." Raymond pressed it into my palm. "I'm going to tack this up on my dorm wall when I get back to school in the fall."

The boys had to get back to work—they still had the stages to set up and the chairs to put out. Orville made me promise to do his likeness at some point during our week at Flausbech.

After I helped Maggie get everything ready in the junior tent for tomorrow's program, I used a large piece of cardboard to create a sign. I painted Doodlebug—Chautauqua's Vagabond Artist in bright red letters, outlined with yellow. Then I added Your Amazing Likeness in Ten Minutes! in black lettering, somewhat smaller. I hoped no one would actually time me. I painted 25 CENTS inside a circle at the bottom. As a border, I drew a number of miniature faces—a variety of shapes and hairstyles—in crayon.

When the parade was over the following morning, I posted my sign on a stake beside my easel and, in my tramp outfit, waited outside the ticket booth between the popcorn stall and the balloon vendor. I had close to an hour before Maggie would need me over in the junior tent.

My first customer was the mayor of Flausbech.

"Awright, sonny, let's see what you can do." He was a man even larger than Ambrose Poindexter, and the legs of the folding chair sank into the earth as he hooked his thumbs on his vest pockets and sat down.

The mayor!

I felt a trickle of sweat forming on my forehead but began working furiously with my blue crayon. A small crowd gathered around to watch, and I was bolstered by the "oohs" and "ahs" that began to surface as I worked in the details and added tints and shading. I knew it would be wise to accent only the first of his double chins, and I made the sparse hair he had combed up over his bald top look like it sprang naturally from his head.

The mayor was pleased and flipped me a quarter. People were lining up now to have me catch their likeness, and I was able to do four more before I had to pack up and head for the junior tent.

During the break between the morning and afternoon programs, I was able to set up again.

"What a wonderful talent!" A portly lady in a huge straw hat and a dress that dripped with chiffon ruffles patted me on the arm.

"Zank you, Madame." I gave her a big smile. "It would be an honour to sketch you."

"Oh my." She blushed with pleasure, easing herself onto the chair.

"Would you care to have zis portrait wiz ze hat or wizout?"

"What do you suggest, Mr. Doodlebug?" the lady gushed.

"Ze hat makes a superb frame for your face, but tilt ze head up just a wee bit."

With each portrait I could feel myself becoming more adept at accenting features that would flatter the sitter. When I was finished, the lady beamed at the results. I'd left out the pouches under her eyes and had used my black crayon to render the grey strands of hair that had escaped from beneath her hat. I'd given her the rosy cheeks and red lips of a younger woman and had included a pearl choker she wore with obvious pride around her plump neck.

The lady pressed fifty cents into my hand.

"My name is Cordelia Van Koopel." She had her hand on my arm again. "I wonder if I might prevail upon you for a very special favour?"

"Madame?"

"Would you be able to come to my home and do a portrait of Pookums? Pookums is my cat whom I love dearly. He's fourteen years old, you know, and very handsome. And, well, I can't think of anything I would prize more than his portrait to hang above the mantel on my fireplace."

"I think it would be possible," I replied, the surprise of the request killing my phony accent for the moment.

"Would you be able to do it after one of the evening shows? I have a season ticket, and I don't want to miss any of the Chautauqua. My house is just a quarter of a mile out of town. Oh . . . and of course, I shall pay you extra for Pookums' portrait. Say, a dollar?"

"Tonight," I quickly agreed.

Cordelia Van Koopel placed a hand on her ample breast as if the prospect of having Pookums' likeness captured was so exciting it was giving her palpitations.

"Walk me home after the show," she said in a whispered aside before she headed for the tent's entrance.

When I looked around, I noticed Scotty had been listening in onto our conversation. He smiled that kind of smile you see on a kid's face when they've just managed to grab the biggest piece of cake on a dessert plate.

The first day's show ran later than it had in Paradise, and I joined the crew boys at the back of the tent to listen to Clementine Cavallero's act. This time Maggie sat at the back with us, and under the electric light, her hair took on a golden glow. As Clementine's last notes faded away, Maggie put her hand up to her mouth. Then Scotty reached over, caught her fingers and held her hand. She smiled at him, and I felt a sharp pang of jealousy.

After the show, as I waited outside the tent, I saw Scotty and Maggie walking arm and arm across the grounds. I gritted my teeth.

"Oh, yoo hoo, Doodlebug!" Mrs. Van Koopel waved her Chautauqua program at me. "Here I am. My, wasn't that an absolutely gorgeous finale! Oh my!" She stopped in her tracks. "You've changed your clothes. Why, you're just a boy!"

"I'm almost seventeen."

She looked me over in that same way I'd seen guys watching girls passing by on Main Street. It made me blush.

Cordelia Van Koopel licked her lips. "Well, you are . . ." She paused, searching for words. "Strapping. A strapping boy."

She linked her arm in mine.

"Hope you don't mind. I have my heels on and that can be hazardous on a dirt road. I like to dress up when Clementine Cavallero is doing her show." Even with a hold on my arm, she managed to shimmy the ruffles on her dress. "Those jewels! I bet the queen of Romania doesn't have any so fine. The stars look like jewels tonight, don't they? And that moon! So romantic."

As we walked along the country road, I felt her grip on my arm tightening, and I wondered how she ever managed in high heels with no one holding her up. In the distance a coyote laughed.

"You're steadier on your feet than Herman was."

"Herman?"

"My late husband. He passed away five years ago. I was . . ." She hesitated and leaned into me. "I was his child bride."

She paid no attention to the choking noise that came from my throat.

"Here we are!" she sang out finally.

The house was dark and squat with one of those porches that ran clear around it.

"Next year they're supposed to be bringing the electricity out to this section and about time, I say. I sure am partial to the idea of coming home at night to a lighted verandah. Running water— now that would be a treat. But who knows when we'll get that."

Inside the house, she quickly lit a table lamp. A large cat with grey and black markings sat watching us from the hallway.

"There he is! Come here, Pookums, and say hello to Mr.

Doodlebug. Him's going to do your portrait, my wittle sweetie pie kittsey."

Pookums got up, stretched elaborately, turned his back on us and strolled away down the hall.

"Oh, you naughty puddy." Mrs. Van Koopel motioned me to follow her as she carried the lamp into the parlour. "We'll just ignore him and that'll have him coming on his little puddy paws to check on us. Curiosity, you know."

While Mrs. Van Koopel fussed around, I sank into a chair and got my paper ready, attaching it to a drawing board I'd fashioned by gluing some heavy pieces of cardboard together.

She arranged the lamp so it cast light on a cushion covered with cat hair that sat like a small plush throne in the middle of a divan. Then she lit a couple of candles on the parlour table. "Does that give you enough light?"

"Well . . ."

"Where is that Pooky? I'll just rub a little teeny bit of catnip on his cushee there. Pookums can't resist that."

She disappeared into the recesses of her house and re-emerged with a tin of catnip to bait Pookums' cushion and a tray with a huge glass of ginger beer and a piece of cake for me.

"Um, thanks," I said. I was thirsty after the long Chautauqua show and our walk afterward. The ginger beer was tangy and cold.

"Pookums! Come and see what Mama has for her widdle sweetie." She put a pinch of catnip onto the cushion and rubbed it in vigorously. "Pookums!"

But Pookums had other ideas and was not showing his whiskers. I found myself stifling a yawn. Mrs. Van Koopel cranked up a gramophone in one corner of the parlour and put on a record.

"This might bring him." She winked at me. "He's very fond of

'Aba Daba Honeymoon.' Herman and I used to dance to this. Do you dance, Mr. Doodlebug?"

A bite of cake lodged itself in my throat. Herman Van Koopel stared down at me balefully from his photograph on the wall.

"Let me get you some more ginger beer."

Halfway through "Aba Daba Honeymoon" and halfway through a second piece of cake, Pookums wandered into the parlour and sniffed the catnip. In an instant he was up on his cushion, writhing around, sending small eddies of cat fur into the parlour air. I watched as it drifted into my ginger beer and the cake's icing. Finally the old cat settled onto the cushion and began licking his front paws.

"There." Mrs. Van Koopel sighed. "Isn't that the perfect picture?"

I moved my chair so I had the best possible angle and, holding the drawing board with my left hand—which only protested a little bit—began my quick sketch in blue crayon. Before Pookums moved, I managed to block in the main patches of pattern on his fur. I drew him looking straight at me, an overweight, arrogant feline on his throne who, I could see, would be the winner in any staring contest. I took my time detailing his hair and overlaid green with a bit of yellow to capture the light in his eyes. Finally I worked in the maroon tint of the sofa behind him and even the stripes on the cushion.

"Oh, Mr. Doodlebug!" In a sweeping movement, the widow Van Koopel clutched her bosom again, knocking what was left of my ginger beer onto her dress.

"Gee . . ." I quickly set the glass upright again.

"Great heavens! Some days I'm so clumsy. Just give me a moment." She hurried away.

Pookums stared at me slyly from his throne.

In no time at all his mistress was back, wearing a silk wrapper. Even in the dim candlelight it revealed more of the widow than I ever wanted to see.

"Gotta go," I squeaked.

"Oh—must you?"

I faked a yawn. "I'm dead."

"Well, let me get your money." As she fished a silver dollar out of her coin purse, her wrapper came loose.

"Oops!"

I closed my eyes.

She pressed the coin into my palm. Her fingers were warm and moist.

"Why don't you have another piece of cake? There's more ginger beer. And we've yet to have our dance." She lowered her eyes and then looked up at me coyly.

I almost dropped the money getting my hand away and I slipped the coin into my pocket as quickly as I could.

"Thanks," I blurted out, as I grabbed my drawing pad and dashed for the door.

The thought of more ginger beer had made me feel as if I was about to burst. So I took advantage of the privacy of a large apple tree at the edge of Cordelia Van Koopel's yard—certain that I was out of sight of her parlour window.

I was sure I could hear the sounds of "Aba Daba Honeymoon" following me out onto the road. It's a song I have no fondness for even to this day.

CHAPTER 13

A few clouds had gathered in the night sky, obscuring the moon as I ran back into town. Although there were other routes to get to the Chautauqua grounds, my boots automatically took me past the rooming house where Maggie and her father and the other Chautauqua players had their quarters. From the alley behind the house, I could see there was a light still on in one of the upstairs gable windows, and I wondered if Maggie was in that room, maybe running a brush through her fine golden hair.

As I stood there, hidden beneath the branches of a chestnut tree, I heard what sounded like a fight down at the end of the alley. I wasn't the only one out past midnight.

The moon broke free from the clouds, and I saw a hulk of a man attacking a much slighter person. And I couldn't help thinking how Albert used to grab me in the same way—so I couldn't use my arms.

"I'm telling you," the smaller man gasped, "I'm paying you what I can. I haven't got . . ."

"You might not have it," the big man growled, "but your lady friend does. I seen her when she's up on stage drippin' with jewels."

"I can't ask . . ."

"But I *can* take . . . and I *will*. You don't want to mess with me. It's not so easy goin' on stage with broken legs."

"Sheamus—please."

There was something familiar about the voice of the man with his back to me. They had moved closer and I could see the big man more clearly now. He had the face of a mangled pugilist—a broken nose, a cauliflower ear and a scar running across his forehead. It looked like he'd slept for the past week in the suit he was wearing.

"Oh—it's 'Sheamus, please,' is it? Seems like I been hearing nothin' but 'please' from you ever since we first ran into one another. 'Please can I have a job helpin' out at one o' yer speakeasies . . . please, I need to borrow some money because my little girl needs an operation for her eyes . . . please . . . please . . .'"

Although he still had his back to me I suddenly knew, without a doubt, that this was Maggie's father. For a couple of seconds no one spoke.

"What was I supposed to do? I didn't know you'd got out of jail."

This was a character I hadn't seen Robert Tremain play on stage. He was struggling for words.

The big man laughed, and it was like rusty nails being pried off a tin shack. "Did you think I was goin' to be in the slammer forever?"

"I *will* pay you, Sheamus."

"Two days. I need the money now."

"That's impossible!"

"You actors . . ." Sheamus laughed again. "Yer good at makin' the impossible happen."

Tremain slowly turned, and I moved behind the tree trunk.

He didn't look back as he climbed an outside stairway to his room.

I thought Sheamus had headed off down the alley, but when I peeked out from behind the chestnut trunk, he was just standing there staring at me.

I took off running. Although I knew I was headed in the wrong direction to get back to the Chautauqua grounds, I figured it would be easy enough to double back. I was more than relieved when I finally got to the park and saw the crew tent with the bulk of the big Chautauqua tent behind it.

"You ol' tomcat," Orville muttered, waking momentarily as I slipped into bed.

"No, please—anything but a cat."

"Huh?" Orville grunted and then went back to sleep.

I had trouble getting out of bed the next day. Raymond finally gave my shoulder a tug and told me I'd better get up before the crowds started pouring in. Our quarters were just a couple of steps off from the main tent auditorium, and I knew Ambrose Poindexter wouldn't be happy about anyone wandering around in his skivvies while people were coming in. I wasn't due to help Maggie in the junior tent until the afternoon, and it would have been a shame to miss collecting some more coins doing crayon sketches.

As I worked at my easel in front of the Chautauqua tent, my mind kept returning to the scene in the alley. How had Maggie's father become indebted to this man—so obviously a thug? Did Maggie know the kind of trouble her father was in? And how much of a lady friend was the bejewelled Clementine Cavallero to Robert Tremain?

It wasn't until we'd finished the afternoon program in the junior tent that I had a chance to get Maggie alone and talk to her. Scotty, who had been hanging around while we cleaned up, had been called to the train station to meet an incoming act for the evening show. For once I was the one walking Maggie back to the rooming house.

"Tell me about the year you had your eye operation," I said. "That must have been an awful time for you."

Maggie stopped for a minute. We were on a walking bridge over a stream that wound its way through Flausbech.

"Awful—that would describe it all right. I don't know what was more awful though—losing my eyesight or Daddy going out of his mind worrying about whether he could get me to a good doctor." Maggie looked down at the trickling water, as if it were a stream bearing memories. "We were lucky. Daddy got some money— quite a bit of money. From an aunt, I think, who'd left it to him in her will. So we were able to go to the best doctor in New York."

"Did you know Clementine then?"

"Oh yes." Maggie smiled. "She was Mama's best friend. We've known her forever. I hope some day she and Daddy get married."

I leaned on the bridge railing beside her. The scent Maggie was wearing made me think of a field of wildflowers. And looking at her next to me, I knew why her father had invented a story to lessen her worries.

"I'm glad you found a doctor," I said.

"Think of it!" Maggie laughed. "What if I'd never had a chance to see you—see what you look like."

"That would've been a real tragedy!"

But she didn't laugh at my little joke—just squeezed my hand as we left the bridge and headed up the hill to the rooming house.

It was a couple of hours before the evening show, so I changed out of my vagabond costume and headed downtown. I wandered along, peering into store windows, checking out the posters at the movie theatre.

"Come in and see the show, sonny?" A woman sitting at the ticket booth smiled at me and cracked the gum she was chewing. "It's *Tarzan*. The shows don't get much better than *Tarzan*."

"I'd like to but I'm working at the Chautauqua."

"Oh—the Chautauqua." She cracked her gum again. "That's where I'd like to be instead of cooped up here in this hot weather and hardly no one coming to see the show 'cause they're all over at the tent in the park."

Next to Flausbech's movie theatre there was a drugstore with a soda fountain. I remembered the last time I'd had an ice-cream soda—the day of Pa's accident, that last half hour when the world still seemed a wonderful place, when it had been possible to let ice cream melt on my tongue while Jimmy talked about what it felt like to pitch the curve ball that suckered Huntsville's last batter.

Suddenly I wanted to feel that ice cream on my tongue again. I went into the Flausbech Drugstore, climbed onto a stool and placed my order.

"Strawberry soda and two scoops of ice cream, please."

As I finished my soda, I twirled around on my stool and noticed that across from me, one half of the Flausbech Drugstore was actually the town's post office. There were mailboxes, a wicket and a bulletin board papered with official-looking notices—including a few WANTED posters. There was one for a couple of bank robbers with a $500.00 reward offered.

When I wandered over to take a closer look, I was stopped dead in my tracks by a picture in the centre of the board. Under the heading of WANTED—FOR HORSE THIEVERY AND PETTY ROBBERY was a photograph of me and the offer of a $50.00 reward.

When no one was looking, I ripped the poster off the board and stuffed it into my pocket. I hurried outside, ducked down a back alley and pulled the poster out to have another look. LEROY BARNSTABLE. My name was in bold print beneath a snapshot that had been taken by Pa on my thirteenth birthday. Albert must have retrieved it from the carpet bag I'd left in the Harvey House in Jackson Junction. But I was sure no one would recognize this little boy, his hair slicked back, wearing a bow tie. Nevertheless, I ripped the photo into pieces and dropped it into one of the garbage cans in the alley.

That night, my sleep was troubled by a dream of Albert and Virgil riding through the Chautauqua grounds shouting, "Has anyone seen this boy?" I was running with just an Indian blanket wrapped around me, trying to escape from them. Albert twirled a rope and lassoed me, dragging me along the ground behind his horse.

"Let me go!" I screamed and woke up to find Raymond shaking me.

"It's okay, Doodle. It's just a bad dream."

"Hey, let a person get some sleep," Scotty grumbled from his bunk.

CHAPTER 14

After Monday's show in Flausbech, Robert Tremain and Clementine travelled on to the other towns on that week's circuit. I wondered if Sheamus would figure out where Maggie's dad had gone and would be there to make good his threat.

I got my answer midweek when I walked by a jalopy parked halfway up on the sidewalk at the edge of the park. There was a man sprawled across the front seat, asleep, snoring, his mouth gaping—it was Sheamus. The driver's door was partly open, and it looked like a sealer jar had rolled out of the car—the kind moonshiners used to sell their wares.

He certainly wasn't hard on Tremain's heels. But I had no desire to be there when Sheamus woke up, so I hurried across the park to the big tent where the Wednesday evening show had been on for about an hour.

As I slipped in, John Caitling Gerrard, the famous orator, was winding up his speech, and I could see the audience was hanging on his every word.

"Times, like shoe leather, can seem tough. Yes, tough. But the worthwhile journey, our movement along any difficult road in the direction of our hopes and dreams, is made on human tenacity and durable soles."

As I applauded with the audience, I felt that his message might have been directed especially at me.

The show finished up with a ventriloquist who got everyone laughing as he argued with his dummy, followed by an all-female string quartet. Poindexter, of course, made one of his appeals for pledges as he bade everyone good night.

When I headed outside after helping the tent boys straighten up, I was relieved to see that Sheamus' jalopy had disappeared.

The junior pageant was a hit once again at the final show. As the children paraded across the stage, said their pieces and sang the songs Maggie had taught them, there was a collective sigh from the crowd. Then, after one of Ambrose Poindexter's farewell speeches—he did three or four during the closing show—the audience settled down to enjoy the closing acts.

The Palace Players' production of *The Warden's Daughter* took up most of the last part of the evening. In the warmth of the tent, some of the audience closed their eyes and caught forty winks while the warden's daughter worked at figuring out ways to free her wrongfully imprisoned lover. But they were quickly knocked out of slumberland when Slats Slewfoot, the villain, began firing blanks from his six-shooter at the warden, who returned his fire.

The audience, fully awake by the time the Palace Players took their curtain call, welcomed the Swiss bell-ringers. Maggie had been sitting with her uncle throughout the show, but she made her way over to where I was standing with the tent boys as the bell-ringers tinkled and clanged their way through their closing pieces. And although she gave me a smile, she ended up standing by Scotty. Orville shrugged his shoulders and shot me a sympathetic look.

Once the audience began streaming out, we sprang into action and started folding up chairs. My wrist hadn't bothered me at all the last couple of days, so I was giving the tent boys a hand. The electric lights were still strung up and gleaming when I noticed a bulky figure entering the tent—Sheamus had finally surfaced.

"Where are you, Robert Tremain? No use hiding!" His words were slurred, oiled by liquor.

Maggie, who was on her way out, was startled and stumbled against him.

Sheamus took hold of Maggie's shoulders and lifted her up, the way a child might lift a rag doll. He roared Tremain's name again, and Maggie yelled back at him, "What do you want with my dad?"

The props from *The Warden's Daughter* hadn't been put away yet, so I bounded onto the stage, grabbed Slewfoot's gun and raced toward Sheamus. "Let her be," I shouted, "or I'll shoot you dead."

In his life of crime, I guess Sheamus must have developed respect for a pistol pointing at him. He released Maggie, and Scotty caught her in his arms. I heard a crashing of chairs as Raymond and Orville ran over to back me up.

"'T ain't none of yer affair," Sheamus grumbled, his eyes steadfast on the gun I was holding.

"Give me the gun, Doodle," Raymond said, "and run as fast as you can to the sheriff's office. Tell him there's been an assault."

"No need." Sheamus' voice had taken on a wheedling tone. "I . . . I made a mistake. I'm on my way now."

"All right, get going," Raymond said, motioning with the pistol toward Sheamus. "Right out of town would be a good idea. If we see hide or hair of you . . ."

Sheamus backed out of the tent entrance and hurried away as quickly as he could make his bulky body move across the Chautauqua park.

Maggie was still shaking as she clung to Scotty.

"What does that crazy guy want with my dad?"

"You get a lunatic or two hanging around wherever you set up a stage," Raymond said. "They're drawn to show business like flies to honey."

"It's a good thing the props for *The Warden's Daughter* hadn't been packed up yet," I said, but my voice sounded a little shaky now too as I thought of what Sheamus might have done, had he realized the gun was loaded with blanks.

"I'll walk you home now," Scotty said. He still had his arms around Maggie.

Orville noticed the expression on my face. "We're going to need you here," he said to Scotty. "Doodle can walk her back."

"But . . ." Scotty sputtered.

"Yeah, the night's not getting any younger." Raymond picked up a couple of the chairs he'd knocked over. "We've still got a ton of stuff to do if we want to have everything loaded before the freight comes through."

Scotty glared at Orville and Raymond as Maggie took my arm and we headed out.

I scanned the grounds and the road next to the park to see if there was any sign of Sheamus. There wasn't.

"Thank you, Doodle," Maggie said, holding on to me as if I were a life raft. "You were wonderful."

She hadn't cried earlier, but there were some tears now. I dug a handkerchief out of my pocket. "It's clean," I said.

That made Maggie laugh, and she took off her glasses and dabbed at her eyes.

"I was so scared," she said.

"I thought you were pretty brave."

Maggie laughed again, but there was a little catch in her throat. "You are the brave one."

She'd quit holding my arm when she took her glasses off, so I slipped my hand into hers now that she had them back on.

She gave me a smile. "I don't really need the glasses at night, but this dress has no pockets."

When we got to the rooming house gate, Maggie kissed me on the cheek.

"I think I'm safe now," she said.

After her kiss, my voice seemed to have gone into hiding, and when it came back, it cracked as I said, "Good night." But it sounded like a grown man's when I added what Ma always said: "Sweet dreams."

When I got back to the tent, Scotty grumbled, "Took you long enough. Did you stop off at Mrs. Van Koopel's on the way back?"

I just smiled at him and called out to Raymond and Orville, "Your muscle man's here. What would you like me to do?"

"Muscle man? Oh, good." Orville tossed me a coil of rope that made me stagger as I caught it.

"All this junk needs to go on the dray." Raymond gestured at the stacked chairs, the tent canvas that needed folding into bags, piles of pegs and poles, and trunks of props. "But first we need to take the stage apart and pile up the lumber."

"That all?" I laughed, and Scotty shook his head as if I'd lost my mind.

The truth was—I had.

———————

CHAPTER 15

We were moving on to another prairie town, Lancaster, Ambrose Poindexter had informed us, giving his head a bit of a weary shake. "Getting money out of sponsors in Lancaster is a Herculean task. We must gird our loins—move like Samson into the pecuniary fray."

Maggie's dad and Clementine came by car with the Quarter Time Quintet, arriving on the Sunday afternoon. As I helped carry their bags into the Lancaster hotel, I noticed Maggie giving her dad a hug that was longer than usual.

"Hey," he said. "You'd think I was gone for a year—not a week!" Robert Tremain grabbed a couple of the bags and turned to me. "How's Doodle?"

"Good, sir. Thank you."

"The sketching? Giving Michelangelo a run for his money?"

"It's good, sir—though I think Michelangelo . . ."

". . . wouldn't have been any good at doing a crayon drawing of a banker's widow." He laughed and gave me a wink.

I was amazed that he wasn't floundering in some kind of slough of despond. How was it possible for him to put Sheamus out of his mind?

Tired as I was after the set-up, I made my way back uptown to the hotel and was glad to find Maggie out on the verandah. She was fanning herself with a palm fan. A porch light did magical things to her hair, which she'd tied back with a ribbon to keep it off her face. She wore a light grey dress that looked as soft as moth wings.

"All finished? I noticed how busy you were putting the fence up when I was getting things ready for tomorrow."

"Yeah—sorry. I was hoping I'd be able to get over and help, but Orville wasn't feeling well and had to lie down. Raymond and I got all the chairs set up." I sank into the opposite corner of the porch swing where Maggie was sitting.

"Did you tell your dad what happened at the closing show?"

Maggie nodded. "He was so upset, I ended up comforting *him* to begin with. He said he thought there was someone—maybe in Chicago—of that description." She sighed. "I really don't want to think about it anymore."

How long would her father be able to avoid telling her that he and Sheamus had dealings? I wondered.

Somewhere in the parlour one of the musicians began playing the piano, and the tinkly, fluttering notes of "Glow, Little Glow-worm" spilled out onto the porch—another of Ma's songs. A huge tabby cat came and rubbed against one of Maggie's feet. As she reached down and began stroking its head, it jumped up into Maggie's lap. I couldn't help remembering Cordelia Van Koopel's Pookums, and the thought made my arms feel itchy.

"Don't you just love cats?" Maggie asked.

"My favourite animal." It was worth a lie to get closer to Maggie on the porch swing.

When Sheamus didn't show up in Lancaster, I heaved a sigh of relief. After Maggie's scare in Flausbech, her father phoned her almost every day from the towns where he was doing his shows.

Gradually my worries about Sheamus faded. Instead I worried about the growing attachment between Scotty and Maggie. I wouldn't allow myself to think of the word "love." But I couldn't help replaying in my mind Maggie collapsing into his arms that last night in Flausbech. Why was Scotty always just in the right place to catch her?

I wished I were tall and blond with the kind of summer tan that Scotty had. Every time I looked in the crew-tent mirror I was reminded that living in my vagabond costume had kept me as pale as the petals of a trout lily. I needed to find time to get to a barber, and I was exasperated by the appearance in the past week of two pimples—one on my nose and one on my chin.

In the breaks between shows, while I was at my easel, Scotty and the other tent boys would be out playing a game of football or scrub with the local kids. And Scotty—especially if Maggie happened to be watching or even taking a turn at bat—would have his shirt off, flexing his muscles.

At times I was discouraged, but my feelings for Maggie spurred me to think of ways to win her affection. I'd pick bouquets of wildflowers to brighten whatever room she was staying in, and sometimes she'd pluck one or two to wear in her hair or as an ornament on her dress.

I bought a scrapbook for her and filled its first pages with sketches showing the events of our Chautauqua summer, especially focusing on anything that might make her laugh—such as Raymond tripping and falling into the watering trough in Lancaster. Or one of the little boys in her junior group bringing his pet skunk to the tent to show everyone. In each new town I'd give her another picture or two.

When I did a crayon sketch of her sitting in her story chair, telling a fairy tale to an adoring audience, she was so pleased that she threw her arms around me. And I felt as if I'd suddenly had a hundred helium balloons attached to my body, allowing me to float into the air. I think I drifted around for most of the afternoon with my feet off the ground—until I noticed Scotty and Maggie walking hand in hand into the Chautauqua tent, and my balloons popped.

"You've got it bad, don't you, kid?" Raymond said as the two of us took our turn doing dishes after supper.

"Yeah—I guess." I scraped out the remains from our stewpot into a bowl we'd been leaving under the table for a stray collie dog that had adopted us. Remembering my barnyard friend from Cutter's Creek, I'd dubbed him "Duke."

"First love?" Raymond asked. "She's a mighty fine girl, our Maggie. I wouldn't mind stepping out with her myself, but I've got a girl back home—and besides, we wouldn't want to drive Maggie crazy with everyone running after her, would we?"

"Is your girl"—I gave the stewpot a rinse, causing Duke to leap away from his bowl when some of the water splashed out onto him—"uh . . . the first one you've ever loved?"

Raymond laughed. "No, I think she's about the fifth. I used to fall in love regularly, about once a year ever since I was fifteen. But this last one, Priscilla, she's the real thing."

"You can tell? I mean, the real thing?"

"Yup." Raymond gave me a playful snap with his tea towel. "Of course, I thought the other four were too when I first started going with them."

Thanks, Raymond, I thought, *that really puts my mind at ease.*

CHAPTER 16

The next few weeks were a blur—one Main Street running into another. Setting up the big brown tent in a schoolyard in Jetson Falls, in the town square at Eddington and in a farmer's field just outside of Moose Point. We moved steadily toward Ashville, our final town.

Ambrose Poindexter had a map of the Chautauqua circuit that he unfolded from time to time, allowing me a look at the route we were taking over the summer. I noticed that it led us in a wide loop that circled back toward Cutter's Creek, taking us to towns along a railroad to the south. A crow could fly from Jackson Junction right over Cutter's Creek and continue on to Ashville in a line as straight as you could draw with a ruler's edge. Albert and Virgil never travelled south to Ashville because the route was troubled by a cluster of lakes and the roads were poor. But it was still close enough that my wrists broke out in a rash as I watched Maggie's uncle tap a pudgy index finger on the last town on the circuit.

"It's a good termination town," he said. "Loyal supporters. You might anticipate, Doodle, that the performers will be drooping a bit following the rigours of many weeks. But the good folks of

Ashville always seem to encourage the opposite—to have us go out in a blaze of glory, as it were."

When we finished our set-up at the grounds of Bertram Ashe's Farm Machinery Works in Ashville, Orville and I accompanied Ambrose Poindexter on a stroll along Main Street. He stopped in front of the Dreamland movie theatre and waved his walking stick dismissively at the display of posters offering laughs and thrills.

"A passing fancy," Poindexter declared. "Have you ever sampled the wares of a nickelodeon? Sad—very sad! Flickering black-and-white images. The human body cut into bits and pieces. Soundless, except for fractured tunes from some out-of-tune piano played by a third-rate musician. And they say this jittery lantern show could be the death knell of the Chautauqua! Do you see me trembling in fear?"

We did not. But later that night I paid a dime and caught the last showing at the Dreamland. One of the reels was a boxing match which, I had to agree, seemed like a poor substitute for the real thing. Then there was a serial called *The Tiger's Tail* with Ruth Roland—outlaws trying to get a young woman's inheritance away from her. This one kept me on the edge of my seat as the heroine faced ferocious jungle animals as well as human villains.

But it was a Charlie Chaplin film that caught me spellbound. Even though I'd never seen a Chaplin movie, and barely any other ones—Pa and Ma had taken me to a couple of films in Spirit Falls when I was twelve—I'd seen photos of Chaplin in the newspaper. I suspect I must have been thinking of him when I assembled my own vagabond outfit. As the little tramp created havoc in a pawnshop, everyone in the theatre was roaring with laughter, and

I couldn't help but feel myself walking in Chaplin's oversized boots with their floppy soles. That could be me up there on the screen; me making everyone laugh. Or maybe one of the cowboys in the serial, galloping across the screen on my trusty horse. I left the Dreamland, shaking my head with the wonder of it.

Somehow Poindexter, despite his size and girth, managed to look cool and collected in Ashville's opening-day parade, with his white hat and a linen suit as bleached as buffalo bones. He held up his walking cane as a baton of greeting to the throng that had gathered. And I was reminded of what a ship in full sail must look like as he sat in the mayor's car at the head of the parade.

Ashville had been experiencing a heat wave for the week prior to our arrival. Despite what Maggie's uncle had said about the good citizens of Ashville, the crowd that lined its main thoroughfare looked a bit tired and wilted, not quite able to rally to the promise of the street banners and the toe-tapping tunes of the Quarter Time Quintet, who mopped perspiration from their brows as they paused between numbers.

As usual, I helped the tent boys hand out leaflets, but our promotional chatter came out in the sauna-like heat as limp as the handkerchiefs most of the ladies kept handy. Men fanned themselves with their hats. One child had figured out how to fold a leaflet with accordion creases so it could be used as a fan. Soon just about every kid along the street was doing the same. Ambrose Poindexter would not be amused, but we couldn't help laughing.

"Don't like the feel of this here heat," I heard one farmer say to another. "Got a heaviness to it that could mean a storm brewing. Recollect a day like this back just before the war . . ."

I took particular notice of Maggie's father and Clementine Cavallero whenever we were doing a first-day program. Their handsomeness as a couple caught the attention of onlookers.

"He's just like Wallace Reid—and she's as pretty as Ruth Roland," I heard a townswoman remark to her husband.

"You and your films!" He laughed. "Let me see actors in the flesh—that's what I say. Give me real live people on the stage like we're going to see tonight."

I had donned my tramp outfit for the parade and set up my easel so everything would be handy for me to begin my sketches when we reached the Chautauqua grounds. In fact I slipped away and ran on ahead as we neared the Farm Machinery Works so I'd be ready and waiting. To my delight, Clementine Cavallero spied me when her touring car pulled into the lot. And once Maggie's dad had helped her down, she made her way over to me. She'd glanced my way the odd time during the summer but had never actually come over to talk to me.

"So you are the artist I've been hearing about?" She smiled.

I decided there on the spot that the woman in the crowd who had compared her to the movie serial queen Ruth Roland had been wrong. Clementine Cavallero was infinitely more beautiful.

"Do you have time to do my portrait?"

"Oh yes, Madame! Please 'ave a seat."

I sketched in her oval face and massed the dark hair where it showed beneath her wide-brimmed hat. She had delicately arched eyebrows and heavy eyelashes. The colour of her full lips made me think of ripe rosehips. I worked furiously, trying to catch all of this with my crayon strokes. I couldn't help noticing that she wore very little jewellery, just some earbobs and a pearl necklace that rested at the base of her neck in a space of exposed skin that made me a little faint.

"It's lovely," she said, when I'd completed it. As she reached into her handbag, I found my voice and declared, "A gift, Madame—please!"

As Clementine Cavallero leaned over and kissed my cheek, I'm sure my face flushed a brighter red than any rouge she wore.

A small crowd had gathered around the easel and applauded at the end of this little scene. It took me a few minutes to gather myself together enough to proceed with the business of sketching the wife of one of the Farm Machinery workers who had bobbed hair and a noticeable overbite.

Hot as the morning had been, the heat of the day increased as the sun sizzled to its zenith across a cloudless sky. I noticed the Anvil Chorus busily rolling up the tent side panels to let in air as I headed over to do my part in Maggie's program with the children of Ashville. Even here, the mugginess of the day was working to make some of the children fretful or listless. One of the younger boys lay down on the grass inside the tent and closed his eyes. I felt like I wouldn't have minded joining him.

When Maggie finished the afternoon program and the children had drifted out of the tent, we sank down onto a couple of chairs before tackling the business of putting things away and readying for tomorrow. Maggie pulled a hankie out of her pocket and dabbed at the beads of sweat that had surfaced along her forehead.

"How'd you like an ice cream soda? It's what Doctair Doodle recommends . . ." I managed to get myself out of my chair, doff my derby and give her a little bow.

"Can't say no to that." Maggie laughed.

Ashville had more than just a soda fountain bar in a drugstore. There was an actual ice cream parlour. It was busy with the Chautauqua crowd between performances, but we were able to get a seat by the window.

This was my idea of heaven, sitting across from Maggie, sipping sodas slowly on the shank of a summer day. I was so busy looking into her eyes that the rest of the world—the hum of chatter from other tables, a player-piano tinkling a tune, the patches of sunlight flitting through the window glass—all seemed to disappear. And there was just Maggie.

"I wish you were coming back to Chicago with Daddy and me."

I drifted back from my dream world and caught what Maggie was saying.

"What are your plans, Doodle?"

"Chicago? What would I do? Where would I live? I need to find work somewhere that'll get me as far away from Albert and Virgil as possible."

"Maybe you could stow away in my trunk!"

As I laughed, the soda went down my windpipe and I choked, making a horrible sound. People at a nearby table looked over and chuckled at me. I felt embarrassed and looked out the window.

I noticed someone going into the sheriff's office across the street. Although I caught only a glimpse of him in profile when he turned to go in, I was certain the man was Albert Grimble.

"Maggie, I've got to get out of here. He's in town . . ."

"The guy who's been stalking Daddy?" She put her glasses on and peered out the window.

"No. Albert Grimble—he's checking in with the sheriff. I was afraid he might show up. I'll have to lie low"

It was actually on my mind to head out of town, but I couldn't bear the thought of missing these last few days of the Chautauqua with Maggie. As long as Albert was in town, though, I knew it would be a good idea to keep out of the public eye.

In the crew tent, Orville was sponging his face and arms from a basin of cool water before changing into his shirt. The tent boys always spent some extra time on their grooming the day that Clementine Cavallero was performing.

"Too hot to cook supper tonight," Orville said. "We're going to grab a bite to eat over at the hotel. You want to come along? I hear they make a great ham sandwich and potato salad."

"Naw, I'm not hungry. I just had something over at the ice cream parlour."

With Orville gone to join Scotty and Raymond downtown, I checked the cigar box under my cot where I'd been keeping the money from my crayon sketches. In every town, I'd exchanged the coins at the end of the week for dollar bills, and it was getting close to a hundred dollars. Enough, if need be, to pay back the money I'd taken from Virgil's rosewood box. Or enough to get me a good distance away by train.

It was too hot to stay in the tent, though, so I stashed the cigar box where I knew I could get to it in an instant, grabbed a sketchbook and headed for a shady spot by the Farm Machinery Works. It gave me a good vantage of a huge oak tree and the town's buildings just beyond, but I'd only blocked in the vista when I nodded off.

I must have slept for a couple of hours because, when I woke, I could see people drifting back to the Chautauqua grounds for the evening show. I grabbed my sketchbook and headed across the yard. The tent boys and Robert Tremain were watching some teams of horses tethered to a hitching rack at the edge of the grounds.

"What's up?" I asked as I made my way over to them.

"Something's spooking those horses," Maggie's dad said. "See how nervous they are?"

"Surely there isn't a bear or a wildcat this close to town." Orville scratched his head.

Raymond took a puff on his pipe, then exhaled a small cloud of smoke. "I think we're in for some weather," he said. "Animals can sense that ahead of everyone else. We'd better be prepared to batten down the hatches this evening. It's easy to get a big blow after a day like this."

It looked like there might be some truth to Raymond's prediction when small gusts of wind began to surface on the Chautauqua grounds just as people were filing in for the evening show.

One farmer took a look at the clouds that had built in the west late in the afternoon, and the greenish cast to the sky, and announced, "Come along, Bertha, kids—get to the wagon quick. We're makin' for home."

"Aw, Pa—can't we stay for the show?" one of his children complained.

Another started crying, but he shooed the whole family ahead of him to the hitching rack as if he were herding sheep out of harm's way.

A couple of other farm families joined suit.

"Now, folks," Ambrose Poindexter said, appearing outside of the tent. "Don't be afraid!" he announced in a voice that seemed to have its own built-in loud-hailer. "Looks like we're in for a bit of weather, but our Chautauqua tents have been designed to stand strong during anything a summer storm can throw at them. The show will be progressing as usual."

"The tent nearly blew down last year at Paradise," Raymond whispered to me. "Stick close by us tonight, Doodle. We might need your help pounding in the pegs if they start to pull loose and lighting lanterns if the electricity goes off."

Despite the building storm, the tent filled up. The listlessness I'd noticed in the crowd earlier seemed to disappear as talk of the weather buzzed through the audience. Strong gusts of air were beginning to blow through the tent now, so I helped fasten down the side panels that had been open throughout the day.

When Ambrose Poindexter got up on stage to welcome the crowd, his appearance was accompanied by a tremendous clap of thunder. Some of the children sitting at the very front screamed or squealed while others giggled. Mothers came up to retrieve a couple of the youngest ones who had begun to cry.

The wind howled and the tent's supports groaned. I saw the tent boys hurrying out and I scurried after them.

"Go to the junior tent, Doodle," Raymond shouted, handing me a sledgehammer, "and pound in the pegs there. We'll take care of the ones around the big tent."

It was hard work with the wind coming in fierce, almost horizontal, blasts that seemed determined to lift me right off the ground. I thought of the tall tale I'd told the kids back in Paradise about being picked up by a cyclone. Maybe the furies were getting back at me. It must have taken me the better part of an hour, but I managed to pound the pegs so they were stuck well into the earth and then made my way back to the entrance of the big tent. As I was about to duck in past the ticket booth, I noticed a car pulling into the lot, its headlights glistening in the rain that had started to fall.

What an odd time to be arriving for the Chautauqua, I thought.

I crouched by the ticket booth and watched as a figure as dark and bulky as a gorilla descended from the vehicle.

Lightning flashed, illuminating Sheamus.

CHAPTER 17

The Quarter Time Quintet was making a noble effort to drown out the thunderstorm with an extra-loud version of "Swanee River" as I made my way back into the tent. Poindexter must have reversed the order of the program for some reason, maybe trying to keep ahead of nature's sound effects. He came out onto the stage as the quintet finished.

"Let's give our Quarter Time Quintet a huge round of applause."

I scanned the audience for Maggie and finally spotted her sitting on the other side of the tent with some of the children from the junior program. One little boy sat on her lap and covered his ears as thunder boomed overhead.

It took me a couple of minutes to get over to her. "I need to talk to you."

"What's the matter? You look like you've seen a ghost," Maggie said when she'd managed to free herself from the circle of children.

"Not a ghost—but that guy I pulled the gun on back in Flausbech. He's on his way over here."

Maggie gasped. "We've got to warn Daddy."

"Where is he?"

"Backstage—getting ready to go on."

She headed for the curtained area beside the stage just as her uncle announced: "And now let me present that master of impersonations, that man with more faces than you'll find in a clock repair shop—the one and only Robert Tremain!"

"Oh no! What'll we do?" Maggie was trying to keep her voice to a whisper but she wasn't succeeding. A woman in the audience put a finger to her mouth and said, "Shhh."

"Where's Scotty?" Maggie grabbed my sleeve, lowering her voice. "And the other boys?"

"I'm not certain, but I think they're back inside. Maybe in the wings, checking on lanterns."

We both looked nervously at the tent entrance, but then Maggie's dad began his show and our attention was drawn to the stage. He was dressed as Dr. Sawbones. There was the sudden sound of rain pelting the canvas. Then hail.

"Hmm . . ." Dr. Sawbones looked up at the canvas ceiling. "Sounds like the gods are gettin' some relief from their kidney stones."

The crowd's roar of laughter was drowned out by two loud claps of thunder. Tremain cowered and covered his head for a moment, then shot back a reply: "All right, I'm aware of patient confidentiality, but I've only shared your condition with about a thousand people."

This time the audience's laughter was uninterrupted by the forces outside.

"Keep an eye on the entrance," Maggie whispered. "I'm going backstage to catch him when he goes for his costume change."

Her father was back on stage in his Indian costume when I saw Sheamus straggle into the tent, cascades of water dripping off his hat and coat. He stood there in shadow, watching the stage, steadying himself against a pole.

I wondered how long he would wait there and where the tent boys were.

Maggie's dad seemed to be scanning the audience while he made his plea as the Indian chief. "Great Manitou, hear me . . ." He stopped mid-sentence.

He must have spotted Sheamus.

While Tremain was changing for his next role, Ambrose Poindexter came out.

"Sit tight, folks." He gestured with his hand to the sea of people in the audience. "It is the twentieth century and man has mastered the elements. Our canvas engineers are standing by in the event of any emergency, which, I hasten to add, is most unlikely to occur. They are making certain our tent poles are secure. Wave to the folks, Raymond . . ."

Raymond was in the middle of the tent where he held one hand against the pole and waved with his other. The audience clapped.

"And, Scott . . . is over there with the east subsidiary pole, and that's Orville over there with the west one."

Another round of applause.

So that's where the tent boys are if we need them.

I didn't take my eyes off Sheamus, though. I knew one of the smaller poles at the entrance was supporting him more than the other way around.

When Robert Tremain came on again—this time as a Scot in a kilt, Maggie ducked her way over to me.

"He's going to stay in the wings close to Clementine," Maggie told me. The audience was laughing over her dad's broad Scottish accent. "For some reason he thinks this guy may be after her too."

When Tremain finished his skits, Poindexter reappeared on stage. "My friends . . ." He raised his arms as if he were giving a benediction. "Better to be inside, listening to the marvellous acts of the most outstanding Chautauqua circuit I've assembled in all of my ten years as superintendent, than out in your vehicles being bombarded by the proverbial cats and dogs. Now, while I have your attention, I ask you to consider pledging your sponsorship for next year's program. You might think it would be difficult to come up with anything more spectacular than what we've assembled this year, but give us the winter months, my friends . . . give us the winter months. And speaking of spectacular . . ." Ambrose Poindexter waved a welcoming hand toward the wing that served as a dressing room, ". . . it is my pleasure now to present the brightest star in our crown of musical gems, the incomparable Clementine Cavallero."

It seemed like the rain let up for a minute or two as she came onto the stage. Electric spotlights flashed off the tiara in her raven hair and danced from her dangling earrings. The jewels on her neck and bosom winked at the audience, suggesting an exotic world of glitter and romance.

Tonight she held a fan of ostrich feathers that wavered gently in her hand as she nodded to the violinist and began singing a song in Italian—a song that dared the storm to intrude on its exquisite beauty. For a couple of minutes I forgot all about Sheamus, and I think Maggie did too. That voice . . . that magnificent voice . . .

And then I looked back. Sheamus' eyes were fixed on Clementine Cavallero—and her jewels—like a wolf zeroing in on the fawn that's straggling behind the herd. He seemed stunned at first, but then he took a step forward and, as he did so, there was another resounding clap of thunder.

All of the lights went out.

A huge groan rose up from the audience, and the children sitting in front cried out.

"No need to distress yourselves. Our able-bodied crew will illuminate our venue momentarily . . ."

I was surprised at how quickly the boys were able to move from being guardians of the tent poles to bearers of light. Within a minute or two, they had placed lanterns on the stage, and Orville had handed me some others to light.

"The show will go on!" Ambrose Poindexter announced.

Clementine Cavallero gave him a nod. "Tonight," she said to the audience, "I was going to sing *to* you, but when it is dark and stormy outside—and it's even a little dark inside— I think we will all feel better if we sing together. That is what my family did when I was a little girl. And here is one of the songs we sang—so please, sing along with me:

> *Daisy, Daisy, give me your answer, do,*
> *I'm half crazy all for the love of you.*
> *It won't be a stylish marriage—*
> *I can't afford a carriage,*
> *But you'd look sweet upon the seat*
> *Of a bicycle built for two.*

The audience joined in heartily and laughed and applauded themselves when they had finished. Clementine led them in singing several other songs, often voicing the less familiar verses solo, but making encouraging movements with her hands for the crowd to join her in the choruses of "On Moonlight Bay," "By the

Light of the Silvery Moon," "In the Sweet Bye and Bye" and "The Sidewalks of New York."

What a versatile performer she was. The audience, singing lustily, seemed to have forgotten all about the storm. And when I glanced at Sheamus lurking at the tent entrance, even he appeared mesmerized by her voice.

Ambrose Poindexter came back onstage with the evening's performers to wish everyone goodnight. The storm had subsided. Thunder rolled off into the distance as people made their way through the muddy lot to their vehicles and wagons or picked their way through puddles back to the town sidewalks. Bertram Ashe, the owner of the Farm Machinery Works, had Ambrose Poindexter in tow.

"Maggie," Poindexter called out, "tell your father I'll catch up with him later at the hotel. Mr. Ashe, one of our esteemed sponsors, and I are going for a late supper."

"Uh . . . sure," Maggie said, heading for the stage.

I had tried to keep track of where Sheamus was but lost sight of him in the crowd. Maggie's dad put his arm around Clementine and had started to usher her off the stage when there was a loud roar. Sheamus flung himself at Clementine. He must have made his way back behind the side curtains and leaped out from there. It was as if he had materialized out of thin air. He grabbed at her tiara and tore some of the jewels from her throat. Robert Tremain tried to pull him off, but with a mighty fling of one arm, Sheamus sent him sprawling.

Both Maggie and I screamed when her dad knocked over a lit lantern as he tumbled. Instantly the spilled kerosene fed flames that began licking at the canvas.

"Fire!" Maggie shrieked.

The tent boys ran for pails of water. Clementine was screaming as Sheamus struggled to rip the choker from her neck. Finally it broke—its jewels flying everywhere.

When the tent boys ran back in, the flames were already dancing up to the paraffin-laced canvas roof and the water had no effect.

"Get out of here!" Raymond shouted.

As Clementine broke free from Sheamus' hold, Robert struggled to his feet, grabbed her hand and raced with her for the exit. "Run—get out of the tent!"

Maggie and I ran out as the flames spread.

"Is everyone out?" Orville shouted.

I looked around. Scotty and Raymond had got out, along with Clementine and Maggie's dad.

But not Sheamus.

I dashed back to the entrance and peered in. I saw Sheamus stumbling around, clutching a handful of Clementine's jewels. He tripped, banged his head against the stage, and lay there, motionless.

"That guy is still in there. Out cold!" I yelled.

"Oh, God." Scotty started toward the entrance—then backed away.

"We can't leave him. Get me some rope!" I shouted.

Raymond cut some rope from the supports at the side of the tent and knotted them together quickly.

"You're crazy if you go back in there," Scotty said, and I felt him grab my shoulder.

But I shrugged off Scotty's hold, snatched the rope from Raymond, and—for the life of me, I'm not sure why—raced back inside. The fire was roaring above me and some bits of flaming canvas were already drifting down. I dashed to the stage, threaded the rope through Sheamus' belt loops and tied a knot. Suddenly a fiery tent pole crashed down in front of me.

This is it. I am going to die in a fiery furnace.

I leaped over the pole and scrambled out of the tent with the rope still in my grasp.

"Pull the rope," I hollered to the tent boys as I collapsed on the wet ground. "Pull as hard as you can."

Raymond and Orville grabbed the rope and leaned back as if they were in a tug-of-war. It seemed to take forever, but before the tent came down in a ball of fire, they had Sheamus' unconscious body on the muddy grass.

Maggie was down on her knees by my side. "Doodle?" She brushed away a lock of hair from my eyes. "Are you okay?"

I looked up at her and the crowd that had begun to gather around us. Two men had pushed themselves ahead to the front.

Next to the sheriff, Albert Grimble stood—a gleam in his one good eye.

———

CHAPTER 18

"That's him, Sheriff," Albert said. "There's the thief." He looked like he was ready to reach down and grab me.

"Don't you touch him," Maggie said, her voice clear and forceful. "Don't you lay a hand on him."

"He's a thieving . . ." Albert sputtered, but he drew back, at least for the moment, from Maggie's fury.

"He's a hero." Her voice was cooler now. "He saved a man's life."

"Make way," the sheriff shouted as two ambulance attendants hurried in with a stretcher.

"Are you okay, boy?" one of the attendants asked, looking down at me.

"I'm fine—the guy who needs help is over there," I said, pointing to where Sheamus lay with the rope still curled around him like a sodden snake.

Albert was shifting from one foot to the other, shaking his head as if a swarm of insects had descended on him.

The Ashville fire brigade finally arrived with sirens blaring. The sheriff began shouting directions to keep the crowd back and clear a path so the firemen could reach the burning tent.

"He's my charge." Albert stepped toward me as I got up.

"Keep your distance," Robert said, blocking Albert's path. "Whatever grievance you harbour against this young man had better wait, sir."

Clementine was standing behind Robert, rubbing her neck. I was struck by how beautiful she looked in the midst of the rest of us all covered with mud and soot. There was mud on her gown too, but somehow you didn't notice it. After Sheamus had ripped off her tiara, her hair had fallen down onto her shoulders, and it hung there now in a dark cascade.

"Uncle Ambrose!" Maggie called. Her uncle was hurrying across the grounds as fast as he could move his portly body. When he reached us he pulled a handkerchief from his pocket and mopped his face, an expression of dismay and horror registering in the light from the flames. For once, he was speechless.

The big tent had collapsed, but the fire was spreading to the junior tent.

"All our stuff is in there!" Maggie said.

Oh no! My money in the crew tent!

The firemen had been able to reach the crew tent with their hoses and were pouring water on it so it had not caught fire. I made a mad dash past Albert toward the tent. He lunged at me, but Robert grabbed his arms and held him back.

I got through the maze of fire hoses, struggled with the dripping flaps and crawled under my cot to retrieve the cigar box.

When I returned, the sheriff was talking with Albert and Maggie's uncle. I couldn't hear what they were saying, but Robert Tremain was giving Albert a couple of pokes in the chest with a finger.

"Oh, Doodle, you're shivering," Clementine said. "We need to get you to the hotel."

Maggie put an arm around my shoulder, and we slipped away with Clementine into the crowd.

A few cars had driven up, ringing the edge of the grounds, and people were watching the fire from their automobiles. Clementine had no trouble convincing a young man in one of the cars that he should take us as quickly as possible to the hotel.

Maggie climbed into the back seat with me. I saw her wipe a couple of tears from her cheek before she busied herself with getting a car robe wrapped around me. Clementine, in the front seat, was continuing to thank the young man, the owner of a haberdashery in Ashville, who joked that it was worth a fire to have such a beautiful and famous singer riding with him in his automobile.

As we drove away, I took a look back at the Chautauqua grounds. There was only the odd little flare of flame now. I closed my eyes, hugged my cigar box to my chest and leaned against Maggie. As the haberdasher had said, some things were worth a fire.

Pa used to say, after a long day of auctioneering, that he was ready to sleep the sleep of the dead. For the first time in my life I think I knew how he really felt. When we got to the hotel, I had some sense of Maggie and Clementine arranging for a room and helping me up the stairs. But I think I was asleep before my body hit any of the bed linens.

As soon as the sun seeped through my window and warmed my bedroom, I was wide awake, reliving all the events of the previous evening. The alarm clock by my bed read ten minutes to five. I quickly got dressed and walked over to the Chautauqua grounds where the tent boys were already raking the ashes and ruined canvas into piles to be carted away.

"I guess that's the end of the Chautauqua for Ashville," I said.

All that was left standing was the crew tent and the canvas fence surrounding the grounds. What remained of the junior tent had been pulled down and heaped into a pile. One of the castle towers from the backdrop peeked out from behind a mess of ruined supplies and costumes and bits of charred canvas. Maggie's piano, its veneer scorched and blistered, rested at a drunken angle, one of its legs caught in a gopher hole.

"Not exactly the end." Raymond stopped his raking for a minute. "The show's going ahead in the high school. Poindexter's been over there most of the night."

"Maggie's program too?"

"That's what they're saying. The main show in the gymnasium, the junior program in the art room."

"Your Doodle costume's okay." Orville gestured toward the crew tent. "Nothing worse for the wear than if we'd been through a heavy rain."

He was right. I changed into some clean clothes and gathered my Doodle costume to put on later at the school—that was if the sheriff didn't arrest me. Scotty was waiting for me just outside the tent door.

"I'm off today," he said. "Catching the train home. There won't be much for us to do once we've finished raking everything up."

"Home?"

"Yup, back to Indiana." Scotty gave me a little smile. "Just wanted to say goodbye and to say"—he stopped for a minute, looking down at his work boots as if he were searching for cues there—"say that what you did was pretty brave, kid. Kinda stupid—but brave."

I was at a loss for words as it struck me that Scotty was giving up more than just these last few days.

"Want some souvenirs?" Scotty asked, reaching into a pocket and pulling out some bits of melted glass with pieces of metal filigree sticking to them. "Clementine Cavallero's jewels. That thug almost got himself killed for nothing better than bottle glass."

"Thanks, Scotty." I rolled the bits of glass in my hand for a minute and then tucked them into my pocket. "Good luck."

I was filled with a mixture of sadness and elation. Soon Orville and Raymond would be gone too. The world that had taken me in was slipping away—and where was I to go? Part of me wanted to grab my cigar box and take to the road before the sheriff and Albert got their hands on me. But another part of me wanted to stay and see if Maggie and I might be able to figure out a way to knit our lives together. It was time to quit running from the Grimbles.

I wondered where Albert was as I trudged back to the hotel. But I didn't have to wonder long. It seemed like the hotel parlour had a delegation waiting for me—Albert Grimble and the sheriff, Robert Tremain, Maggie and Clementine, and Sheamus with a large bandage around his forehead.

I was surprised to see Clementine standing beside Sheamus' chair with a hand on his shoulder. For someone who'd been through what we'd all been through, she still had the appearance of a rose in full bloom. She'd pinned her hair back up, and her neck—unbedecked by any jewels—was graced by a silk flower nestled between the collars of her summer dress.

"Mr. McGarrigle," she said, "I'd like you to meet the boy who saved your life. This is Doodlebug . . ."

The slightest of blushes deepened the pink in her cheeks, and I realized that she must never have heard my actual name.

"My stage name," I said.

Sheamus lumbered up out of the chair and I felt his powerful arms enfold and embrace me.

"My boy . . ." For a moment he held me tight, and I felt like I was in the grip of a grizzly bear. "What can I say?" His voice broke. "What can I say?"

After he released me, he pulled out a pocket handkerchief and dabbed at his eyes. I couldn't think of anything to say at first. Images of Sheamus threatening Robert Tremain, shaking Maggie and pulling Clementine's jewels off flashed through my mind.

Why had I gone into that burning tent?

"I only did what any man . . ." My voice choked on the word *man*.

Maggie reached over and squeezed my shoulder. It was a squeeze that seemed to say, *Yes, you* are *a man.*

Remembering the bits of melted glass in my pocket, I retrieved them and held them out as an offering to Clementine. "All that's left of them," I said. "Your jewels."

Sheamus looked down at what I was holding.

"You mean they was fake?"

Clementine smiled ruefully. "They made a good show."

"Enough of this!" Albert stood up and gestured to the sheriff.

"Hold your horses, Mr. Grimble," the sheriff said, turning to Clementine. "I understand Mr. McGarrigle assaulted you, Miss Cavallero, and you, Mr. Tremain. You both have the right to lay charges."

"It was a misunderstanding." Clementine gave the sheriff a tiny smile. "I think it's all cleared up now."

"We had some business dealings," Robert Tremain added. "But it's all sorted."

Sheamus nodded.

"Then the fire was not a deliberate act?" The sheriff raised his eyebrows and looked at Maggie's dad.

"Yes, the fire was an accident," Robert Tremain said.

Now the sheriff turned toward Albert. "And you, sir?"

"This boy . . . the fact is he's a runaway. He stole money and a horse . . ."

"That money was rightfully mine. It belonged to my ma!" I hated the tremble that had crept into my voice, and I was afraid that tears were just waiting at the edge of it all.

"Money and a horse, I said!" Albert's body puffed out with righteousness.

"A horse?" The sheriff gave me a stern look. "That's serious."

"I only rode it a little ways, and he took it back."

"You have the horse?" the sheriff asked Albert, sounding annoyed.

"Yes, but . . ." Albert sputtered.

"You were in your cousin's charge, son." The sheriff turned to me. "What made you run away?"

"There was no kindness . . ." Now the tears had started to come, and I brushed angrily at them with my hands.

"From what I hear, this boy's been nothing but reliable." The sheriff cleared his throat. "And, with the fire last night, I'd say downright heroic."

"All the same . . ." Albert stepped toward the sheriff who waved him back.

"How much money did he take?" the sheriff barked.

"Ninety-nine dollars and that was only half of what he owed

me," I said. The room was silent for a minute. "I can pay it. I've got my drawing money."

"I ain't got a hundred on me but I got fifty," Sheamus said, pulling his wallet out.

"And here's the rest—from Clementine and me," Robert Tremain said, counting out five ten-dollar bills from his pocket.

The sheriff took the money and counted it carefully in front of Albert. "Now you might want to make yourself scarce. I've been hearing about how you treated this boy, and if you've been keeping back what's rightfully his—well, I might be getting in touch with Sheriff Andover in Jackson Junction. I think Cutter's Creek is in his jurisdiction."

"I don't want your money. I want the boy to pay! It's the principle!" Albert laid the wad of bills on the parlour table beside him.

"There's a hundred dollars there. You take it or leave it," the sheriff said.

"I won't be taking it. It's the principle."

"That's settled then," the sheriff said, "and I don't want you bothering this young man any more, hear?"

He gestured toward the hotel door and Albert left.

"Thank you, sheriff," I said. "That's a great relief."

The sheriff nodded. "Now, you folks, I'm guessin' are needed down at the high school for setting up the Chautauqua. Think I'll take in the afternoon show m'self."

At the high school we put everything we had into making the program fun for the children. They were all excited about the fire, and it was a challenge getting them to think about anything else.

We had the use of the school's art room so we were able to get them working on costumes for their pageant.

When the last of the children had filed out at the end of the afternoon program, Maggie flopped into the art teacher's chair.

"I think this has been the longest day in my life," she said.

"Did your dad . . . did he tell you . . . about Sheamus?"

"You knew, didn't you?"

"Not much. Just his name and that they knew each other . . . and that your dad owed him money for your eye operation."

Maggie sighed. "I can understand why Daddy didn't want me to worry about the money, but I wish he had told me about Sheamus."

I reached over and put my hand over Maggie's. "So have they finally sorted everything out?"

"I think so. Daddy said Sheamus was like Lazarus today, but he wasn't too sure who he might be tomorrow—especially if he begins drinking again. But Daddy left him with a handful of post-dated cheques. At the end of the year we won't owe him anything." Maggie leaned back in her chair and closed her eyes. "And to think I started all of this. A white cane would have been a lot less expensive."

"Oh no, Maggie, don't ever think that."

"I'm so glad you're here right now and I can see you." She opened her eyes and smiled at me. "And I'll be able to see Clementine in her wedding dress."

"They're getting married? When?"

"End of September—the date's set. And you're invited."

She reached over and took my hand, and I suddenly felt light-headed.

"Scotty's gone." The statement just popped out of my mouth from nowhere.

"I know. He came around to say goodbye before he caught his train."

She was silent and seemed far away for a moment. I thought she must have been thinking of their time together over the summer. But then she came back from wherever she'd gone, leaned over and kissed me.

"You're coming home with us, Doodle," she said.

The world shifted a little on its axis.

Home.

It'd been so long since I'd had a home I wasn't sure what the word meant anymore.

"Okay," I said. No word had ever sounded so inadequate.

"Okay?"

We both began to laugh.

And the only way to stop was to kiss her back.

EPILOGUE

Yes, Pa would have called the year I turned fifteen a topsy-turvy year. When I think of how low I felt with Ma's passing and the prospect of a continued stay with the Grimbles, stumbling into the Chautauqua the summer of 1923 was something I feel providence may have lined up for me. If you believe fate takes a hand in the fortunes of men.

I had lost a family, but that summer I found another one, and, in time, Maggie and I built on that family. Children. Grandchildren. And great-grandchildren. But I'm getting ahead of myself. You're probably wondering what happened when Poindexter's Chautauqua circuit closed that year.

With the first touches of fall colour tingeing the trees and bushes along the railway, we headed to Chicago. It turned out that we wouldn't be spending the winter there, though. Robert Tremain had been spotted by a talent scout from the movies in one of those towns where we'd pitched the Chautauqua tent.

"You know how I feel about those flickering photographs," Ambrose Poindexter sighed over a cigar when his nephew broke the news to him. "But, my boy, if California beckons, heed its call and find out the shape and nature of that seaside siren. Your job with the Chautauqua awaits you, should you need it."

In one of those odd turns of fate, it was Clementine Cavallero with whom the motion picture camera fell in love. By the time we moved to Hollywood, she was Mrs. Robert Tremain. But it was her stage name we saw on movie posters, and when we watched her on the screen, it was as if we were watching someone who surpassed being human. She seemed to glow from somewhere inside herself, and all the emotions imaginable stirred in her large, mascara-rimmed eyes.

The irony was, of course, the movies were silent so no one heard the beautiful voice that had held us in such thrall on many a Chautauqua evening. Robert Tremain never became a matinee idol, but he did play character parts in films for many years. In one picture he even played his wife's grandfather. In another, he portrayed a villain who kidnapped her and bound her to a chair in a burning house.

And me? I became a scene painter—storm clouds over Hawaiian palms, sunsets streaked across desert tableaus, palaces of Arabia— huge canvasses against which movie actors played their roles.

Maggie's uncle had been wrong about film. More and more movie theatres were springing up in the prairie towns and cities, elaborate picture palaces with velvet curtains, gilded swirls of plaster with paintings on the ceilings and walls. More and more homes had radios too, where music that people had once travelled miles to listen to in our Chautauqua tents was there with the turn of a button. Ambrose Poindexter, who struggled over the next two years to keep his summer tents filled, passed away in the same year that many of the Chautauqua circuits died—1925.

And what of Maggie . . . you ask. She tried the movies too,

with the prompting of her father and stepmother. But her eyes could not tolerate the searing Klieg lights. She was happier anyway attending teacher's college and becoming a teacher.

When our own children were scattered across that spectrum of ages—Bobby, six; Amber, eight; and Marilyn, ten—we made a trip back to Cutter's Creek. I was able to rent a car in Jackson Junction, and we drove out to the small cemetery where Ma was buried. Someone had been keeping the weeds at bay, and Amber, who had an artist's eye, arranged the flowers we'd brought, in a glass jar by the tombstone.

Nearby there was another grave.

ALVINA GRIMBLE. BELOVED WIFE AND MOTHER. 1859–1931.

Was it my imagination, or did I hear the whisper of a couple of voices, one sweet and true, one quaint and wavering, singing "Rock of Ages, cleft for me . . ."?

The children splashed in Cutter's Creek, and we picnicked along the bank, the way Ma said she had once done. We even drove by the farmhouse on our way back. It had become as old and dry and grey as the surrounding fields—and I chose not to stop.

The Great Depression had come, and there would be hard years ahead for the people who had once watched our Chautauqua shows. But I knew in my heart that it was possible to persevere and move on.

As that Chautauqua orator once said, "Times, like shoe leather, can seem tough. But the worthwhile journey, our movement along any difficult road in the direction of our hopes and dreams, is made on human tenacity and durable soles."

AUTHOR'S NOTE

As a child, I found I could spend many hours poring over the contents of a trunk in which my grandmother kept many of the treasures of her lifetime—photos and letters, old calling cards and picture-postcards, the christening gowns of babies long since grown to middle age, buttons and belt-buckles and bits of lace, dress patterns, locks of hair tied with ribbon. One item in particular caught my fancy, a poster which, when you unrolled it, announced the repertoire of my grandfather's half-brother, Robert H. B. Tremain, an actor with the Chautauqua and Lyceum circuits. The family knew him as Ben, but on this poster, his name had taken on some embellishments befitting a performer of note. There were a number of photographs on the poster. Beneath a studio photo showing him in his regular dress of a natty suit, stiff collar and tie, were several pictures of him in the guises of the characters he portrayed on stage—an ancient man with a long white beard, a Highlander, an Indian with a full headdress, and even an old lady. I was a child who could spend a good deal of time living out of a costume box so the fact that someone in my family had managed to do this for a living intrigued me no end.

We have a letter from Great-uncle Ben, written from Kentucky when he was on the Lyceum circuit in 1912, in which he expressed how much he missed his parents and his brothers, who had moved to Canada and settled in Alberta, as well as his own wife and daughter in Sioux City, Iowa. It was the last letter the family received. Robert H. B. Tremain mysteriously disappeared and was never heard from again. He was something of an adventurer, as ready to strike out and go prospecting for gold or join a hunt as appear before the footlights of a Chautauqua stage. Perhaps he tried his luck prospecting in Mexico, where, during this time of turmoil, he might have been killed. No real hint of what actually happened to him has ever surfaced.

It was Tremain's Chautauqua poster that spurred me to write the story of Doodle and his summer with the Chautauqua circuit, and, in it, I pay homage to Robert H. B. Tremain by inviting him to materialize as Maggie's father. I can't help thinking he would have enjoyed the chance to be under the canvas of one of the big tents again.

The Chautauqua tent shows that travelled from town to town throughout the United States and Canada in the early decades of the twentieth century grew out of the Lyceum movement that thrived in the latter part of the nineteenth century. It was a movement dedicated to bringing culture to Americans who had little access to educators and entertainers. Carl Sandburg, Booker T. Washington and Mark Twain were among the Lyceum's speakers. In 1904, the idea of taking such week-long shows to small towns by using tents and daily programs that rotated from one place to the next over the period of week was given a trial run. The circuits chose the umbrella name of "Chautauqua," from the New York Chautauqua Institution, which offered summer-long

146

programs on theology, literature, science and the arts—a model for what the travelling tent shows were aiming to do. The circuits grew in popularity, especially as the programs expanded to include an increasing variety of entertainments—bands and popular singers, opera soloists, magicians, ventriloquists, plays, character impersonators, and comedians.

Chautauqua programs in each town relied on a good deal of involvement from the town populace. A Chautauqua Committee of locals, working with a Chautauqua advance agent, had to gather pledges and guarantee the cost of putting on the program. A junior program, run by a Chautauqua "story lady" or "junior girl," involved the children of those attending, often culminating in a pageant to be put on in the big tent at the end of the week.

As movies grew in popularity in the 1920s and radio became a staple in more and more homes, the Chautauqua circuits faded away.

The geography of the Chautauqua circuit in *The Runaway* is fictional. So are the performers and acts for the shows, but these, of course, are shaped from a study of what someone in a Chautauqua audience might expect to see and hear in 1923.

ACKNOWLEDGMENTS

I am indebted to these sources for providing me with details of the Chautauqua and its circuits:

Chautauqua in Canada by Sheila S. Jameson, in collaboration with Nola B. Erickson. Glenbow Alberta Institute, 1979.

Culture Under Canvas: The Story of the Tent Chautauqua by Harry P. Harrison (as told to Karl Detzer). Hastings House, 1958.

The Romance of Small-town Chautauquas by James R. Schultz. University of Missouri Press, 2002.

T hanks to David Stephens and Michael Katz, my scrupulous editors.

GLEN HUSER

Glen Huser's novels for young readers have been highly praised and won a number of awards. *Touch of the Clown* was a Mr. Christie Silver Award winner; *Stitches* won Canada's Governor General's Award for Children's Literature in 2003 and Alberta's R. Ross Annett Award; and *Skinnybones and the Wrinkle Queen* received a Governor General's Silver Medal in 2007. A teacher and librarian for most of his life in Edmonton, he has retired in Vancouver, where he continues to write, pursue his artwork and coach students working on their own books for young people.

You may visit Glen at www.glenhuser.com